Wed in W

Do You Take This Maverick? by Marie Ferrarella

A Conard County Baby by Rachel Lee

A Randall Hero by Judy Christenberry

The Texas Wildcatter's Baby by Cathy Gillen Thacker

The Bull Rider's Son by Cathy McDavid

SHIPMENT 2

The Cowboy's Valentine by Donna Alward

Most Eligible Sheriff by Cathy McDavid

The Lawman Lassoes a Family by Rachel Lee

A Weaver Baby by Allison Leigh

The Last Single Maverick by Christine Rimmer

A Montana Cowboy by Rebecca Winters

SHIPMENT 3

Trust a Cowboy by Judy Christenberry

Million-Dollar Maverick by Christine Rimmer

Sarah and the Sheriff by Allison Leigh

The Cowboy's Homecoming by Donna Alward

A Husband in Wyoming by Lynnette Kent

The Comeback Cowboy by Cathy McDavid

The Rancher Who Took Her In by Teresa Southwick

SHIPMENT 4

A Cowboy's Promise by Marin Thomas

The New Cowboy by Rebecca Winters

Aiming for the Cowboy by Mary Leo

Daddy Wore Spurs by Stella Bagwell

Her Cowboy Dilemma by C.J. Carmichael

The Accidental Sheriff by Cathy McDavid

SHIPMENT 5

Bet on a Cowboy by Julie Benson
A Second Chance at Crimson Ranch by Michelle Major
The Wyoming Cowboy by Rebecca Winters
Maverick for Hire by Leanne Banks
The Cowboy's Second Chance by Christyne Butler
Waiting for Baby by Cathy McDavid

SHIPMENT 6

Colorado Cowboy by C.C. Coburn
Her Favorite Cowboy by Mary Leo
A Match Made in Montana by Joanna Sims
Ranger Daddy by Rebecca Winters
The Baby Truth by Stella Bagwell
The Last-Chance Maverick by Christyne Butler

SHIPMENT 7

The Sheriff and the Baby by C.C. Coburn
Claiming the Rancher's Heart by Cindy Kirk
More Than a Cowboy by Cathy McDavid
The Bachelor Ranger by Rebecca Winters
The Cowboy's Return by Susan Crosby
The Cowboy's Lady by Nicole Foster

SHIPMENT 8

Promise from a Cowboy by C.J. Carmichael
A Family, At Last by Susan Crosby
Romancing the Cowboy by Judy Duarte
From City Girl to Rancher's Wife by Ami Weaver
Her Holiday Rancher by Cathy McDavid
An Officer and a Maverick by Teresa Southwick
The Cowboy and the CEO by Christine Wenger

THE RANCHER WHO TOOK HER IN

TERESA SOUTHWICK

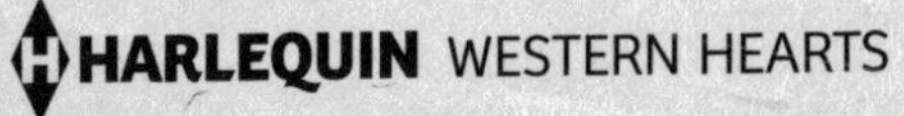

Recycling programs for this product may not exist in your area.

ISBN-13: 978-1-335-50776-1

The Rancher Who Took Her In
First published in 2014.
This edition published in 2020.

This edition published by arrangement with Harlequin Books S.A.

For questions and comments about the quality of this book, please contact us at CustomerService@Harlequin.com.

Harlequin Enterprises ULC
22 Adelaide St. West, 40th Floor
Toronto, Ontario M5H 4E3, Canada
www.Harlequin.com

Printed in U.S.A.

Teresa Southwick lives with her husband in Las Vegas, the city that reinvents itself every day. An avid fan of romance novels, she is delighted to be living out her dream of writing for Harlequin.

To my female friends.
Your support and love inspire me every day.

Chapter One

It wasn't often a woman walked into the Grizzly Bear Diner wearing a strapless wedding dress and four-inch satin heels.

If Cabot Dixon wasn't seeing it for himself, he'd have heard pretty quick because people in Blackwater Lake, Montana, talked and this was something to talk about. The bride had parked a beat-up truck out front and she was a looker. The woman, not the truck. From his seat at the diner counter he had a view of Main Street and had watched her lift the floor-length cream satin skirt in one hand, probably to avoid tripping because it was way too late to keep it from getting dirty. Then she marched inside, as opposed to down the aisle.

He was sitting on a swivel stool, and she slid between the two beside him to talk with Michelle Crawford, the diner's owner, who was openly staring.

"I'm here about the Help Wanted sign in your window."

The bride was even prettier up close, with light brown, blond-streaked hair and a figure that could back up traffic for miles. And that wasn't all. Her voice had the barest hint of huskiness that could stop a man's beating heart for a second or two.

There were a few customers in the diner and everyone continued to stare when the newcomer added, "I could use a job."

"Okay." Michelle slipped him a help-me-out expression, obviously wondering if he would jump in, considering he was the one looking to hire.

When he'd put the Help Wanted sign in the diner window, she'd promised to run interference and weed out the applicants who weren't really serious so he didn't have to come all the way into town from the ranch every five minutes. Frankly, he was looking forward to seeing Michelle handle this one on her own.

Because there was no groom in sight, the lady clearly was a runner. It would appear that, unlike his ex-wife, she'd cut out *before* taking vows and getting pregnant.

Cabot glanced at her flat belly in the tight, unforgiving, dropped-waist gown that wouldn't hide even an extra ounce of fat, let alone a bump. He couldn't swear there was no baby on board, but it didn't look likely. Her bare arms were super toned and she had great shoulders, slender but strong. She was a little lacking in the chest department, but her cute nose and even better mouth made up for it.

The bride rested her palms on the red Formica counter. "I've never waitressed before, but I'm a fast learner and a hard worker—"

Michelle held up a hand. "Let me stop you right there. I'm not hiring, just handling the interviews for the rancher who is." She glanced at him. "The ranch is about ten miles outside Blackwater Lake."

"I see." The woman looked momentarily thrown, and then she nodded. "I admit I didn't read anything on the poster after the *help wanted* part and that doesn't speak well about my attention to detail. But I'm a bit distracted just now."

Cabot figured that was the truth. The wedding dress was a big clue.

"Well—" Michelle gave him another jump-in-anytime look. "The job is for a summer camp counselor. The owner runs a program for kids at his ranch, and duties include activities, sports and whatever else comes up. General pitching in as needed."

"I can handle that," the bride said. "I love kids."

"I'm not sure you're what he had in mind."

"Who?"

"The rancher who's looking to hire," Michelle responded. "You're probably overqualified."

"I just want to work." Cabot saw something vulnerable and fragile in her expression. "These days a lot of people are taking jobs they're overqualified for and happy to have them."

She was right about that, he thought. Although the job he needed to fill was more suited to a young college kid or recent graduate, he'd posted the sign in the diner window later than he usually did. Camp was starting soon and most people who wanted summer work had already lined something up. That meant he couldn't afford to be as picky as usual.

Michelle folded her arms over her chest and looked the woman up and down. "Even your average employee doesn't go formal to apply for work."

"So you noticed the wedding dress." The bride's tone was deliberately casual, as if she always showed up for a job interview in a long white gown. "I guess I stand out like a fly in milk."

"Pretty much," Michelle agreed.

The woman was plucky, Cabot thought. He'd give her that. Taking a sip of cold coffee, he listened intently, interested to hear what she had to say.

"The truth is, I ran out on my wedding."

"Really? Could have fooled me." Cabot knew he should have stayed out of this conversation but just couldn't resist. "So you broke some poor guy's heart."

She met his gaze and took his measure. "And you are?"

"Cabot Dixon. Couldn't help overhearing. So, why did you run?"

"Not that it's any of your business, but he's a lying, cheating, scumbag weasel dog."

"That sounds bad," he said. "But I have

to ask—couldn't you have said something to him before he showed up for the wedding?"

"Probably I should have. My sister warned me, told me he hit on her, but I was stubborn and didn't believe. Then I caught him kissing one of my bridesmaids at the church. It seemed like an excellent time to let him know the marriage probably wasn't going to work out." She clenched her teeth and a muscle jerked in her delicate jaw. "I hate it when my sister is right."

"Jerk," Michelle said, the single word dripping with disgust.

Cabot had to agree.

"I gave him back the ring with a fervent wish that he'd choke on it, but dealing with the rest just then was—" The bride sighed and the movement did amazing things to a chest that suddenly didn't seem so lacking. "I grabbed the truck keys and left. Drove all night and this looked like as good a place as any to stop."

"It is a good place, honey." Michelle patted her hand and gave him a glance that begged him to take over.

"What's your name?" he asked.

"Katrina Scott. Kate." She glanced between him and Michelle. “Why do you keep looking at this guy?”

“I keep looking at this man because he’s Cabot Dixon, the rancher who put the Help Wanted poster in my window. Take over anytime.” Michelle settled a hand on her hip and met his gaze. “In my humble opinion, Kate is just your type.” To the bride she added, “He’s a sucker for hard-luck cases.”

“I know you mean that in the nicest possible way,” he said to Michelle.

“Maybe I did. Maybe I didn’t.” She smiled at the bride and said, “My work here is done. By the way, I’m Michelle Crawford. It’s nice to meet you, Kate. Welcome to Blackwater Lake, Montana.”

“Thanks.” After the other woman left, Kate turned to him. “You could have said something about being the rancher in question before I spilled my guts.”

“You were on a roll,” he said.

“Just so we’re clear, I’m not a hard-luck case. And I don’t suppose there’s a chance that you could overlook or forget everything I just said?”

“Probably not.”

“I didn’t think so.” She sighed.

“So Katrina. Like the hurricane.”

"I came first and I'm pretty sure my parents named me after a Viking queen or at the very least a Swedish princess."

He laughed. She was quick-witted. He liked that. But Michelle was probably right about her being overqualified. He would guess her to be in her late twenties and likely on a career path that had been interrupted by running out on her wedding. Although by the looks of the ancient truck out front, she didn't have much money.

"Nice dress."

"Thanks. I plan to burn it." She smoothed a hand over the curve of her hip.

The gesture drew his attention and suddenly his mouth went dry. This was a pretty strong reaction and he didn't much trust the feeling, but there was no reason to read anything complicated into it. He was a guy and she was a pretty woman. That was all. But she was looking to work for him and he was looking for a reason to turn her down.

"You need a job."

"It would help me out."

She had pride. He understood and respected that.

Cabot pushed his empty plate and coffee

cup away. "Like Michelle said, it's really a nowhere job."

"Just where I want to be."

"The kids' activities include sports—basketball, baseball, soccer."

"I'm athletic." He noted conviction in her voice, not so much in her expression.

He couldn't tell about athletic, but she looked as if she was in great shape. "I'm offering minimum wage, and that's not much more than gas money for a college kid who's willing to work."

"I'm obviously not a college student but definitely not afraid of hard work. And money buys gas whether you're in school or not," she said. "I'm sensing hesitation on your part and just want to say that you're not seeing me at my best right now."

He had to disagree with her on that. What he saw was pretty darn nice, although she did look tired. She had dark circles under her eyes. Green eyes, he noted. Beautiful, big green eyes.

"When was the wedding supposed to be?" he asked.

"Yesterday."

The skirt of her dress had deep creases, as

if she'd been sitting for a long time. Behind the wheel of a crappy old truck.

"Where did you sleep last night?"

"I didn't."

He'd guess she was running on fumes. "Do you have a place to stay here in Blackwater Lake?"

She shook her head. "Not yet. Maybe you could recommend something."

Glancing out the window, he assessed her ride. The paint was old and chipped, and rust showed through in some places. It had seen better days. He figured she probably couldn't afford to pay for a room.

"Blackwater Lake Lodge is the only place in town, but it's expensive."

"That's okay. I'll be all right."

Again, that was probably pride talking. Sleeping in the truck wasn't a good idea, but she likely had no other choice. She was here without a lot of options. And somehow he felt she was now his problem, which he didn't like even a little bit. Bottom line was the camp needed an extra pair of hands and the duties weren't rocket science. He couldn't afford to be too choosy.

He stood up. "The job comes with room and board. Meals included."

She blinked those big green eyes at him. “Are you hiring me?”

“Subject to approval by Caroline Daly. She manages the camp for me and also does the cooking.”

“Wow. I don’t know what to say.”

He didn’t, either. If anyone had told him he’d be hiring a runaway bride that day, *crazy* would have been the first word that came to mind.

The thought made him irritable. “Do you want the job or not?”

“I want it.”

He looked at the dress then met her gaze. “Do you have anything else to wear?”

“No.”

“You’ll need stuff. I can give you an advance—”

“That’s okay. I can handle it.”

“Okay.” He wasn’t going to argue. “Michelle can tell you where the discount store is and give you directions to the ranch. Like she said, it’s about ten miles outside of town. When you’ve got what you need, meet me there.”

“Thank you, Mr. Dixon.”

“It’s Cabot.” He looked at his watch and shook his head. If he didn’t leave now he’d be late picking Tyler up from school. "I have to go."

"Okay." She held out her hand. "It's nice to meet you, Cabot. I promise you won't regret this decision."

Time would tell. He shook her hand and the electricity that shot up his arm made him regret not letting Michelle handle the interview solo. But the diner owner was pretty close to dead on about one thing. He was a sucker for hard-luck cases. At least he wasn't a romantic sucker anymore.

When a wife walked out on her husband and infant son, it tended to crush the romance out of a man.

A few hours later, as Kate Scott was driving to the ranch, she figured a rush of adrenaline was the only explanation for the fact that she hadn't passed out and run off the road into a ditch. She'd never been this tired in her life. As an athlete she was trained to eat well, get enough sleep and take care of her body. In the past twenty-four hours she'd done none of the above. Candy bars and coffee were nothing more than survival snacks. That was what happened when you drove from Southern California to Montana in nineteen hours.

But the adrenaline rush in the diner had been unexpected. It had a lot to do with Cabot Dixon, she thought as she drove Angelica, her brother's ancient truck, through his gates and beneath a sign that announced Dixon Ranch and Summer Camp.

Serenity was the first thing she noticed. It was all about rolling green meadows crisscrossed by a white picket fence. Majestic mountains stood like sentinels in the distance. As the truck continued slowly up the long drive, she passed a huge house. It looked a lot like a really big wooden cabin with dormers and a double-door front entry. The kind of place *Architectural Digest* would have on the cover for an article about mountain homes for the wealthy.

Following the instructions Michelle Crawford had given her, Kate drove past a real working barn, then a smaller barnlike building with a large patio and scattered picnic tables. That must be where camp meals were served. Beyond that were six spacious cabins. Michelle had told her the first five housed campers and senior counselors, and the last one, a much smaller cabin, would be where she'd stay for the summer. *If* she got the cook's approval for the assistant-counselor position.

She parked by cabin number six and turned off the truck's ignition before blowing out a long breath. What a relief to just be still. It felt weird. Not good; not bad. Just…strange. She couldn't remember the last time she hadn't had a million things going on at once. Training, practice, competition and product endorsements made for twenty-hour workdays. Now she had…nothing.

Sliding out of the truck, she noticed a little boy running toward her. Oh, to have that much energy, she thought.

The dark-haired, dark-eyed kid skidded to a stop in front of her. He looked about seven or eight. "Hi. I'm Tyler, but most people call me Ty. Not my teacher, though. She believes in calling kids by their given name."

"I'm Kate Scott. Nice to meet you, Ty." His features and the intensity stamped on them were familiar. "I bet your last name is Dixon."

"It is." His long-lashed eyes grew bigger, as if she'd read his mind. "How'd you know?"

"You look like your dad."

"That's what folks say."

And when he grew up, he'd probably be just as drop-dead gorgeous as his father. It hadn't escaped her notice that Cabot Dixon was one fine-looking man, which had probably sparked the unexpected blast of adrenaline at the diner. She hadn't been too tired to notice that he wasn't wearing a wedding ring.

She'd felt only a little shame about the spurt of gladness following the observation. Shame because mere hours ago she'd been on the verge of getting married and now she was scoping out commitment symbols, or lack thereof, on the handsome rancher. It felt wrong to ask this little boy about his mother, so she didn't.

She looked around and saw the lake just past a grassy area beyond the cabins. "This is a nice place you've got here, Ty."

"It's not mine. It's my dad's." His expression was solemn, as if he'd been taught to tell only the absolute truth. "He told me to come down and let you know he and Caroline will be here in a few minutes." The boy thought for a moment, as if trying to remember something, and then his expression changed. "Oh, yeah. And I'm s'posed to welcome you to the ranch."

"Thanks. That's very sweet of you. I'm here for the camp-counselor job—to do whatever I'm told to do, which could be dishes. And I'm fine with that."

Ty nodded sympathetically. "I have to do that all the time."

"Even grown-ups have to follow orders."

"Not my dad." She heard pride in his voice. "He gives 'em."

"I guess you can do that when you're the boss," she agreed. "I appreciate the welcome. Thanks."

Thin shoulders lifted in a shrug. "My dad would say that's just the way it is here in Blackwater Lake."

For a second Kate felt as if she'd ridden a twister to the land of Oz. This was a place where folks made a person feel welcome because it was just a small town's way. That was unbelievably refreshing.

"Well, a stranger like me thinks it's pretty cool to get a friendly welcome."

"Where are you from?" He looked up, and a ray of sunshine slicing through the tree leaves made him squint one eye closed.

"I've been all over."

That was vague but still the truth. She trained wherever there were facilities for skeet shooting. Then there were competitions all over the country, all over the world, not to mention the Olympics. Winning had opened the door to lucrative product-endorsement deals, and fitting in those location shoots with everything else was stressful and challenging.

Ted, her too-good-looking-for-his-own-good manager and weasel-dog ex-fiancé, had pushed hard to get it all in and now she knew why. Marrying her would have punched his meal ticket for life. The sleazy jerk had been using her. She'd been stupid to accept his proposal and move forward with wedding plans, but at least her instinctive judgment about the man had been right on target. She'd never once been swept off her feet when she kissed him.

"My dad said you're pretty." The kid was staring at her, obviously trying to decide for himself if it was true.

"He did?"

Ty nodded uncertainly. "Caroline asked if you were as pretty as Michelle said. That's Mrs. Crawford. She owns the Grizzly Bear Diner."

"I met her." And obviously word about the weirdo in the wedding dress was spreading. "Your dad said I'm pretty?"

He thought about that. "He just said 'yes' when Caroline asked if you were as pretty as Mrs. Crawford said."

That was something, anyway. Kate would

have figured if he thought anything at all, it was mostly questioning her sanity for asking for a job while dressed for her own wedding.

"That was very nice of your dad. Thank you for telling me, Ty."

"It's the truth. My dad says you should always tell the truth. People get hurt when you don't."

She was curious about the moral and personal lesson that was in there somewhere. Maybe she'd find out, and maybe she wouldn't. And maybe she was better off not wondering about it at all.

"Here comes my dad and Caroline." He pointed, then raced back down the road to meet them.

Kate watched the man stoop down to his son's level and put a big hand on the small, thin shoulder. He smiled and affectionately ruffled the boy's dark hair before Ty continued running toward the house. One picture was worth a thousand words, and the one she'd just seen said Cabot Dixon loved his boy a lot.

She waited and watched the two adults walk toward her. Now that she'd seen the ranch, something about it pulled at her, and she wanted very much to stay for a little while. It wasn't hiding out, she assured herself. Just taking a much-needed break.

Kate had always thought she was different from other women, so it was surprising to realize that she was having a clichéd reaction as Cabot approached. She found something inherently sexy about a tall, well-built man in worn jeans, white long-sleeved cotton shirt, boots and a black cowboy hat. What was it about a cowboy? He stopped in front of her and again she could *feel* adrenaline obliterating her exhaustion.

A quirk turned up one corner of his mouth. "I sort of miss the dress."

"It's carefully packed away."

"I thought you were going to burn it."

"Something to look forward to." Kate glanced down at the new sneakers, jeans and red scoop-necked T-shirt she'd purchased at the big discount retail store in Blackwater Lake. "This is more practical. And comfortable."

"Amen to that." Caroline looked to be somewhere in her fifties. She was tall with stylishly cut and discreetly streaked blond hair.

"Kate, this is Caroline Daly." Cabot looked from her to the other woman. "Caroline, meet Kate Scott, Blackwater Lake's own runaway bride."

"It's a pleasure." Caroline held out her hand.

Kate gave it a firm squeeze. "Very nice to meet you. And, just so you know, I had my reasons for leaving that toad at the altar."

"Cabot told me." Sympathy brimmed in her blue eyes. "He also said you need a job."

That wasn't technically accurate, but she did need to keep busy. She didn't know any other way to be. "I could use work."

"Have you ever been involved with kids?"

She'd mentored some of the girls in her sport and roomed at the Olympics with a younger archery competitor, but she had never coached. Then Ty's words echoed in her mind. *My dad says you should always tell the truth. People get hurt when you don't.*

"I've never worked with kids. But I was one once," she said hopefully.

"Funny how that happens," Cabot said wryly. "I don't know what I'd do without Caroline. Not only is she a good cook and outstanding camp manager, she's great with kids. Probably has something to do with being Blackwater Lake High School's favorite English teacher and girls' basketball coach."

"Wow. That must keep you busy." Kate had had tutors in high school and had never attended traditional classes with other kids.

Sacrifices were required at the level she competed and she'd never regretted it. Not until she found Ted kissing another woman on the day of their wedding and realized he'd been playing her for a fool.

Caroline waved a hand as if it was nothing. "I like to be busy. I like to cook. Mostly I like the kids, and being around them keeps a person young."

"So that's your secret to looking so youthful," Cabot teased.

Kate tapped her lip and studied the older woman. "Not a secret so much as embracing an attitude. In addition, I think you just have some good genes, the kind of DNA that makes forty the new thirty."

Caroline grinned. "You're just saying that so I'll give Cabot the okay to hire you."

"Busted." Kate shrugged. "But seriously, you look timeless."

Caroline seemed pleased at the compliment. "If I were you, Cabot, I'd hire this young woman. Now I've got to get home and fix dinner for my husband. We own the sporting-goods store in town," she added. "Food has to be on the table at a certain time so someone at the store can cover for him."

"I see." And if her husband looked through

the outdoor magazines that were probably displayed at the checkout counter, there was a good chance he'd seen her picture in an ad for camping and outdoor equipment.

"'Bye, Caroline. See you next week when the kids get here," Cabot said, watching her walk down the dirt road to her car parked in front of his house.

When he looked back at her Kate asked, "So, what's the verdict?"

He reached in his jeans pocket, pulled out a brass key that probably unlocked cabin number six and handed it over. "I'm willing to give you a chance."

"Thanks." Relief swept through her and took the last of her energy with it. Suddenly she was so tired she could hardly stand. Not even close proximity to this handsome hunk of cowboy could generate enough adrenaline to hold back a yawn. She shook it off and said, "Sorry. That's not what I usually do at an interview."

"The first part was bizarre enough, what with the dress. And now it's technically over since you got the job." Sympathy softened his dark eyes before he shook it off. "Caroline's a good judge of character."

"And you're not?"

His mouth pulled tight for just a moment. "I wanted her opinion since she has to work with you. I just sign your paycheck."

A dozen questions raced through her mind, but the one she really wanted to ask was *Does that mean I'll never see you?* The deep disappointment generated by that thought was bewildering; she'd spent barely ten minutes in this man's presence.

"I like her," Kate said. "Caroline."

"Me, too. A lot. So don't make me regret giving you the job." He turned and started walking away. Over his shoulder he said, "Get some sleep. You're going to need it."

A shiver skipped over her as she stared at his broad shoulders. They tapered to a trim waist and a backside that would earn ten out of ten points from any female judge. But she'd learned her lesson about looks being shallow and superficial. She didn't know Cabot Dixon from a rock. It was entirely possible that he used women and threw them away. Just like the man she'd almost married.

Still, the attraction was just strong enough to make her hope that when the summer was over she didn't regret taking this job.

Chapter Two

Two days ago when Kate had arrived in Blackwater Lake after driving for nearly twenty-four hours, doing nothing had seemed like heaven. Now she was rested, restless and bored. She sat in her one-room cabin that was comprised of a small stall-shower bathroom, full bed and kitchenette that had a four-cup coffeemaker, frying pan and microwave. She was grateful to have four walls, a roof and the small cozy space they made, but the smallness was starting to close in on her along with the realization that she'd run away from everything and everyone in her life.

A walk before dinner seemed like a really

good idea. After, she would head up to the big house and talk to Cabot about doing chores to earn her keep until camp started.

She left the cabin and, as a precaution, locked the door. The ranch was remote and quiet and she didn't have much to steal, but you could never be too careful. The beauty of Blackwater Lake lured her down to its edge, where she drew in a deep breath of sweet, clean air. Blue water sparkled where rays of sunshine kissed it, and on the other side, tree-covered mountains stood guard over the serenity.

"So this is what peace looks like," she whispered to herself. It felt as if a louder tone would violate Mother Nature's sensibilities, and that seemed like a sin.

When she'd looked her fill, she went the other way, past her cabin and the ones that campers and seasoned counselors would occupy in a couple of days. She was looking forward to that, to being busy. With too much time on her hands it was difficult not to obsess about how stupid she'd been to accept Ted's marriage proposal.

What a huge mistake she'd nearly made. And how anxious her parents had sounded when she'd called to let them know she was okay but refused to say where she was now. She needed time by herself, and God bless them, they understood. They had handled canceling the wedding and reception and were returning gifts. She had planned to take the summer off for a honeymoon and settling into married life. Now she had time off to figure out where her life went from here.

The sound of a deep voice followed by childish laughter carried to her. Then she heard a muffled slap. As she made it to the top of the hill, she saw that in front of the big log-cabin house Cabot was playing catch with Tyler, who had his back to her. When the boy missed his father's underhanded toss, the baseball rolled downhill toward her. He turned to chase it and stopped short when he spotted her.

"Hi, Kate." His smile was friendly and he seemed happy to see her.

"Hey, kid." She stopped the rolling baseball with her foot, then bent to pick it up.

She couldn't remember the last time she'd played any sport involving a ball. Once she'd started going to the shooting range with her father and showed an aptitude for skeet, her life had changed. Practice and competitions dominated her life. Before that she'd gone to traditional school, where organized peer activities were possible, but she'd never participated. All the family moves because of her father's military career had made her reluctant to join anything. Then she found her best event. The sport, and being good at something, had made her happy. Until finding skeet shooting, she'd never fit in anywhere.

"Are you going to stare at that ball all day or throw it back?" It wasn't clear whether Cabot was irritated or amused.

"Sorry." She drew her arm back and tossed the ball at Ty. At least that had been her intention. It went way to the right of the mark and rolled away from him. "Sorry," she said again.

"It's okay." Ty ran after it.

"Athletic? Really?" One of Cabot's dark eyebrows rose questioningly. "You throw like a girl."

"At the risk of stating the obvious, I *am* a girl."

"Yeah. I noticed."

Nothing in his tone or expression gave away what he was thinking, but Kate remembered that Cabot had said she was pretty. It had been indirect, an answer to a question from someone else, but he'd agreed. That was something and she would take it. Her ego had recently taken a hit, even though it was stupid to care what Ted thought. If she'd been enough, he wouldn't have been hitting on someone else on the day of their wedding.

Ty ran back with the ball clutched in his hand. "Wanna play catch with us, Kate?"

"I don't have a glove."

"You can use mine," Cabot offered. "It's probably a little big but should work okay."

She could have said no, but that eager, friendly, freckled eight-year-old face wouldn't let her. Ty was a sweet kid and his father had taken a chance on a stranger and given her a job. The world wouldn't end if he fired her now for misrepresenting her skills, but she didn't want to go back to Los Angeles and the glare of the spotlight waiting for her there. At some point she'd have to, but not yet.

"Okay, Ty. But you might be sorry. I'm not very good."

"My dad and I can give you pointers."

"I'd like that."

When she moved close to Cabot and smelled the spicy scent of the aftershave still clinging to his skin, the sport of baseball slipped right out of her mind. Everything about him was sexy, from the broad shoulders to his muscled legs covered in worn denim. She liked his white, cotton, long-sleeved snap-front shirt and decided he wore the cowboy uniform really well.

She took the seen-better-days leather glove he held out and put her fingers inside, finding it still warm from his hand. It seemed intimate somehow and tingles tiptoed up her arm, put a hitch in her breathing.

"Ready, Kate?" Tyler called.

"Yes." She dragged her gaze from the man and turned it on his son. "Go easy on me."

"I will. Don't worry. Just keep your eye on the ball." Obviously Ty had heard that advice before.

She did as he suggested, but as it came at her, she didn't know whether to hold the glove out like a bucket or lift it and close her hand around the ball. In the end she jumped out of the way and let it fall.

"That's okay," Ty called. "Good try."

Probably he'd heard that from his father, too. Children were a reflection of their environment, and she had to conclude that Cabot Dixon was providing a very positive one. The revelation made her like him a lot.

She picked up the ball, then straightened to meet Cabot's gaze. Amusement glittered there and his silence said what her mother had always told her three children—*if you can't say something nice, don't say anything at all.*

She put the ball in the glove, testing the feel of it. After several moments, she prepared to throw it back. "Get ready, Ty. I can't guarantee where this is going."

The boy set his sneaker-clad feet shoulder-width apart and held up his glove as a target. "Right here."

The body movement to make it go there was so different from sighting a moving clay pigeon. She was also pretty good with a bow and arrow. During Olympic training, she'd made friends with one of the female archers who had given her pointers in their downtime. Right now she had to command her arm to throw this ball at just the right velocity and close to the vicinity of the kid's glove.

She threw and it went way to the side, out of his reach, forcing Ty to chase after it again. "I'm sorry."

"I like to run," he called out cheerfully.

"Hmm" was all Cabot said.

She wasn't sure whether she was just a little embarrassed or totally humiliated for being proved a fraud. When Ty returned, he moved closer and tossed the ball underhand, like his father had. She turned her hand up but misjudged and it fell at her feet.

"Hey, kiddo, I'm really sorry. This isn't my best sport. Playing this with me isn't much fun for you, is it?"

"It's okay." He shrugged. "You'll get better with practice."

They kept at it for a while, and Kate figured Tyler had also learned patience from his father in addition to encouragement and liberal praise. She actually caught a few and was getting the hang of throwing more accurately. Finally shadows started creeping in and Tyler announced he was getting hungry.

"It's about that time," Cabot said. "Ty, you go on in and wash up for supper."

"Okay, Dad. See you later, Kate."

"'Bye." She watched the boy run up the steps and into the house, then handed the glove back to Cabot. When he started to turn away, she said, "Can I talk to you for a minute?"

"Sure." He folded his arms over his chest. "What's on your mind?"

"I want to do something to earn my keep until the kids arrive for camp." Because that sounded a little like a come-on, she felt it necessary to put a finer point on the statement.

"Chores. Like housekeeping maybe. Cleaning. Doing dishes. Cooking."

"You know your way around a stove?"

"I'm not the best, but I'm definitely competent in the kitchen."

"I already have a housekeeper." He looked as if he'd rather be kicked in the head by a horse than let her into his house. "Although I do my own cooking. You'll earn your keep soon enough. Making dinner for us isn't necessary."

"It is to me. I don't take something for nothing. Cooking a meal would be a way for me to give back."

She was still processing the fact that he had a housekeeper, which made her pretty positive that he was a bachelor. That along with the fact that she hadn't seen a woman at the house or another vehicle besides his truck.

Surely the women around here would be interested in a man as attractive and sexy as Cabot Dixon. The fact that he was single didn't speak well of Blackwater Lake females. Although, by definition, a relationship required two interested parties, which could mean he was unreceptive to being part of a couple. Could be he'd learned the hard way, just like she had.

If Kate had paid attention to her instincts, she wouldn't have gotten herself in this mess. But when she took in the beauty of his land, as messes went, this was an awesome place to be in one.

Something wouldn't let her drop the offer and she was pretty sure the determination was driven by her need to prove she had other skills. That he shouldn't be sorry he'd hired her.

"Do you love cooking?" she asked.

"Not really."

"Wouldn't you like a break from it? Hang out with Ty for a change? Maybe play a game with him?"

"He's used to hanging out on his own." But his mouth pulled tight at the words.

"Sometimes it's good to shake up the routine when you can." She'd certainly done that, and only time would tell whether or not it was a good thing.

"Look, Kate, I really appreciate the offer—"

Before he could say "but," she interrupted and started past him toward the front steps. "Okay, then. Lead the way to the kitchen and I'll get started."

Kate half expected him to stop her either with words or physically. Instead he mumbled something, and she didn't try very hard to understand what he'd said. Then she heard footsteps behind her.

She took that as a yes and walked into his house.

It was weird to see a woman in his kitchen.

Cabot remembered the last time a female, other than his housekeeper, had stood in front of the granite-topped island. His wife, Jen, had said she was leaving him and her infant son. She'd hated the ranch and right that second Cabot had hated it, too.

Now Katrina Scott was here and he hated to admit that she was stirring up more than fried chicken and macaroni and cheese. She was scraping off a patch on the ache in his gut, the yearning for that time when he'd had a whole and complete family. How stupid was it that this woman did that to him? She'd freely admitted running out on a life like that. Although, if he was being fair, the cheating jerk had deserved it.

But here she was, cooking. He'd planned chicken for dinner, but his method involved a boxed coating and the oven. Hers involved flour, egg, oil and a frying pan. His mouth watered at the aroma. She'd rummaged through the fridge and pantry, coming up with all the ingredients necessary for macaroni and cheese. He'd kept her company, just making small talk, because it didn't seem right to leave her in here alone.

Ty ran into the room. He'd been watching TV in the family room, which was an extension of the kitchen. It was a big, open place where he'd once pictured a bunch of kids playing while he and Jen watched over them from the kitchen. That dream went out the door with her.

"Is dinner ready? I'm starving," the boy said.

Kate moved to the stove and checked the chicken sizzling in a pan. "This is done."

After turning off the burner, she lifted the golden-brown pieces to a platter and set it on the island beside a warming tray. Turning, she went to the oven, opened the door and took out a casserole dish using protective mitts. She was better with them than the baseball glove, and the thought almost made Cabot smile.

"The mac and cheese is bubbling nicely. I'd say it's done." She set the dish on the hot tray beside a pot containing cooked green beans. "Dinner is ready."

"Ty—"

"I'm already washed up."

"Okay, then. You're all set, men. Enjoy your dinner. I'll see you tomorrow."

Cabot was just about ready to breathe a sigh of relief as she started to leave. He felt edgy around her and was looking forward to letting his guard down and relaxing. "Thanks for cooking."

"Wait," Ty said to Kate. "You're not eating with us?"

"No, sir," she said. "I'm on the payroll and not doing anything to earn it. That's why I cooked. I certainly wasn't looking for an invitation to stay."

"But, Dad, we should invite her." Dark eyes, eager and innocent, looked into Cabot's.

Apparently his son wasn't getting his vibe about wanting her gone. "We shouldn't take up any more of Kate's time. She probably has things to do."

"She just said she wasn't doing anything and that's why she cooked dinner," Ty pointed out. "You always tell me to be polite and neighborly."

Cabot looked at Kate, giving her a chance to jump in and say she couldn't stay. The expression glittering in her green eyes said she knew he was squirming and she didn't plan to do anything to help him out. If he had to guess, he'd say she was enjoying this.

He always did his best to be a good example to his son, which basically left him no choice. "Would you like to stay for dinner, Kate?"

"I'd love to," she said brightly.

"Cool. I'll set the table. It's my job." Ty proceeded to get out plates and eating utensils and set them on the round oak table in the nook.

"Don't forget napkins," Cabot reminded him. He looked at Kate. "What would you like to drink? Water, iced tea, beer, wine?"

"Beer," she said after thinking about it.

For some reason her choice surprised him. "You look more like a wine woman to me."

"Beer sounded good. I don't drink normally when I'm in—" She stopped short of saying what she was in. Then she added, "I just don't drink much."

He wondered about the slip but let it pass. The less he knew about her, the better off he was. After pouring milk for Ty and grabbing two longnecks from the fridge, the three of them sat down to eat.

"This is my favorite dinner." Ty took a big

bite out of the chicken leg he'd picked off the platter. "This is really good. Way better than the Grizzly Bear Diner."

"I'm glad you like it," she said.

Cabot took a bite of his piece and found the crunchy, juicy flavors unbelievably good. After trying the mac and cheese he decided she was two for two. Green beans fell into a category of not good, not bad. Just something he had to eat because of that being-a-positive-role-model-for-his-son thing.

"Don't you think this is the best dinner, Dad?"

He looked at the boy, then Kate. "It's really good."

"Thanks." She looked pleased.

"How did you learn to cook like this?" he asked.

"My mom taught me. I spent a lot of time hanging out in the kitchen with her."

"Why? Didn't you have any friends?" Ty asked.

"Ty," Cabot scolded. "That's nosy and rude."

"It's all right," Kate said. "You're very perceptive, Ty. I actually didn't have any friends."

"Why?" Ty started to say something, then stopped.

Knowing his son, Cabot figured he'd been about to ask if there was something wrong with her. His son was developing a filter between his brain and his mouth. Maturity was a wonderful thing.

"When I was growing up," she said, "my dad was career army and we moved every couple of years. It got hard to make friends and leave them, so I just stopped. I hung out at home mostly."

"Wow." The boy set his picked-clean leg bone on the plate, his eyes growing wide. "I wouldn't like moving away from C.J. He's my best friend. And I've never lived anywhere but here."

"The ranch has been in the family for several generations," Cabot explained.

Kate looked wistful. "I've never had roots. You're lucky, Ty, to have a long-standing connection with the land and community."

"It's a blessing and curse," Cabot said.

"How so?" She scooped up a forkful of macaroni and delicately put it in her mouth.

"When you're the only son of a rancher, you pretty much know what your career is going to be when you grow up. What's expected of you. There's not a lot of choice."

"Did you want to take another career path?" she asked.

"I majored in business in college because it was expected that someday I'd run this place. What I didn't expect was having opportunities in the corporate sector. That life pulled at me some. But when it's a family business, the situation becomes a lot more complicated."

Kate glanced at Ty, and it was clear that she wanted to ask how he fit into the scheme of things, considering Cabot's mixed feelings. When his boy grew up, would he be expected to take over the ranch? Cabot hoped he would be more flexible than his own father and let his son decide what he wanted to do with his life. He didn't plan on pressuring Ty and saddling him with expectations of taking over the operation. Being stuck on the land near a small town in rural Montana could be limiting.

It was a great place to grow up, but there was a big world out there, and once upon a time it had tugged at Cabot. Now he just didn't think much about it. He was doing his best as a father, rancher and businessman who was exploring the responsible use of mineral rights on the land. Pretty much he was content with things now. Until meeting Kate, that was.

"So, I've been looking over the camp curriculum," she said, changing the subject.

Cabot was grateful to her because taking over the ranch wasn't something he wanted to discuss in front of his son. The years were going by too fast, but a decent amount of time was still left before any decisions needed to be made.

"Caroline takes care of that."

"You don't have input?"

"I could, but I mostly just stay out of the way."

Kate looked surprised at that. "I see."

"You look surprised. Is there a problem?"

"No. It's just that you're so patient and comfortable with Tyler, I'd have thought you were more involved with the camp and the visiting kids."

"I don't have a lot of time for it." Guilt pricked him because he could make more time if he chose. "What do you think of the activities?"

"There sure are a lot of them." She looked thoughtful. "Arts and crafts. Water sports, which makes sense with the lake right here. Archery. Horseback riding. I like that the kids can choose what activities they want to participate in."

Cabot hadn't made any changes since he'd taken it over from his father. And he didn't get involved very much after the kids arrived, leaving it to Caroline to run things day to day.

"They're encouraged to try as many activities as possible," he said, recalling his manager's recommendations. "But it's still their choice what they do."

Kate nodded thoughtfully. "I noticed there was a course in wilderness survival."

"Presenting the basics is wise, although it's up to the staff to make sure the kids' survival is never in question."

"Very funny." She took a sip of beer. "Seriously, though, are basics enough? You always hear stories in the news about someone getting lost in the woods, stranded with their car, driving off the road. Last winter there was the case of a family who got stuck when they went to play in the snow."

"What happened to them?" Ty asked.

"The father did everything right. They stayed with the vehicle, burned the car's tires to stay warm, and everyone huddled in the car at night to share body heat when the temperature dropped below freezing."

Cabot's attention perked up at the body-heat part. His definitely cranked up at the thought of keeping her warm. It was an image that popped into his mind without warning or permission. Once there it seemed disinclined to leave.

"It took a couple of days, but they were finally found not too far from their home." She looked at Cabot. "By the way, I'm certified to teach wilderness-survival techniques."

In spite of the fact that she was doing a good job on her beer, it was hard to believe this girlie girl could hold her own in the wild. "You're serious?"

"Don't judge me by the way I handle—or mishandle—a baseball. I can build a fire without matches and find food in the woods."

"Why?"

"Why not?" she shot back.

He waited for more details, like why she would go out of her way to acquire that kind of skill, but she stared him down without saying more. It made him curious, but he didn't ask. She probably had her reasons for not sharing more personal details. It was typical of all the strays who had a need to use his spare cabin.

All he knew was that she'd been engaged to a guy, then ran out when it was time to commit. Her story was that he'd cheated, but

Cab didn't know for sure. What he did know was that there were too many similarities to his ex, and that was plenty of reason to keep his distance.

But obviously he was cursed. Otherwise he wouldn't be attracted to a woman who had run away from something.

Chapter Three

It was a spectacular night.

At about nine o'clock, after cleaning up the pots and pans she'd used to cook dinner, Kate sat on the wooden bench on the small front porch of her little cabin. The inky-black Montana sky glittered with stars, a sight that took her breath away. The absence of Los Angeles nuisance light revealed the beauty a person couldn't see in the big city.

Being away from L.A. was having unexpected effects on her. She hadn't been this relaxed in a very long time. Dinner with the Dixon men had been partly responsible for that. Fried chicken, mac and cheese and beer were probably the world's most comforting foods. But the best part was that no one wanted anything from her. She'd had to make a federal case to get her boss's permission to cook.

Cabot Dixon was a brooder, which only added to his appeal. He didn't have a poker face, either. That was for sure. When he'd talked about missed career opportunities, she'd seen resentment and resignation in his expression. But when she'd gone into Blackwater Lake to shop for food and toiletries, everyone she'd talked to had said he had made the Dixon ranch more successful than his father or grandfather had. So it might not be his first choice for making a living, but he was darn good at what he did.

The scrape of boots coming down the dirt path startled her in the still night. Adrenaline kicked up her heart rate; she was all alone out here. As a tall form moved closer, lights mounted on the cabins revealed that it was Cabot.

"Evening," he said, not slowing his stride.

He was going to walk right on by. If he'd said nothing, a case could be made that he hadn't seen her, but he clearly had and didn't want to talk to her.

Kate knew she should let him go, but for some reason his remoteness kicked up her contrary streak. She didn't like being ignored. On top of that, she was curious about why he was out here. Surely he didn't exercise. He was lean and muscular, walking proof that his job kept him fit without having to add a workout routine.

"Hey, wait up." She stood and hurried after him.

"What?" he asked over his shoulder.

Kate caught up to him, but it wasn't easy. His long-legged stride made it a challenge. "That's what I'd like to know. Why are you out here? Is something wrong?"

"Nope. Habit. I do a nightly inspection of all the ranch buildings."

"Where's Ty?"

"In bed." Cabot glanced down at her. "He's old enough to be left by himself for a few minutes."

"I wasn't judging," she protested.

"Maybe not out loud, but I could hear you thinking about it."

Just a little. Possibly.

When he got to the grassy area by the lake, he turned right on the dirt path and headed for the barn and corral. He wasn't saying anything, and she felt the need to fill the conversational void.

"It's a beautiful night."

"Yeah."

"Do you ever get used to it? Take all this for granted?"

"Probably."

The least he could do was throw her a bone, she thought. But she didn't discourage easily. A person didn't win Olympic gold medals by giving up when the going got tough.

"The lake is spectacular during the day, but with the moon shining down, it just takes your breath away." Or maybe she was breathless just being near him and trying to match his strides. "The mountains are gorgeous, too. And the air." She drew in a deep breath. "So clean and fresh."

"You're not wrong about that."

"This is a lovely piece of land you've got here."

He glanced down again. "Sounds like you love the outdoors."

"Who wouldn't?"

"My ex-wife, for starters."

Their arms brushed and she could almost feel the tension in his body, the annoyance he felt at letting that slip out.

But he had let it slip. "You were married."

"A lifetime ago."

"What happened?" That was nosy and probably rude, but he knew about *her* past. Turnabout was fair play. This was the opening she'd been waiting for, and she didn't plan to let it drop.

"She didn't like it here. Wasn't happy being a wife and mother."

"That pretty much sucks."

"Pretty much," he agreed. But there was a harsh edge to his voice.

"Must be hard on Ty—not having a mom, I mean." Moments of silence dragged out after the comment, and she didn't think he was going to answer.

"He asks questions," Cabot admitted. "And I answer as honestly as I can."

"What do you say?"

"That the two of us are a different kind of family. But there's no way a kid can understand why his mother didn't want to stay for her own son. Hell, *I* don't understand."

Anger had given way to wistfulness in his tone and that made her wonder if he still had feelings for the woman who'd walked out on him. "Is there a chance that Ty's mom will come back?"

"Always, I suppose."

Kate was a little surprised when he didn't add that it would be a cold day in hell before he took her back. "What if she did?"

His mouth pulled tight for a moment, but when he answered, his voice lacked any emotion. No anger, regret or sadness. Just matter-of-fact. "If she showed up at the front door tomorrow, Ty wouldn't have to wonder where his mother is."

"Do *you* wonder?"

"No. I know where she is." *And she doesn't want to be here.* He didn't say it, but the words hung in the air between them.

"Where is she?" That question *was* out-and-out nosy. Every time he answered something, more stuff popped into her head to ask him. At some point he was going to tell her to mind her own business, but until he did she couldn't seem to stop herself from inquiring.

"Helena."

Montana's capital. "So it's not that she doesn't like Montana."

"Nope. Just the ranch and small-town life."

"Does Ty know how close she is?"

"Nope. She hasn't shown any interest in

seeing him and I wouldn't put him through that unless she did." He slowed his pace. "There's no point in it. Rejection hurts."

"Yeah." She'd been rejected very publicly. She was realizing that she didn't love her ex-fiancé because he hadn't crossed her mind all that much since she'd arrived in Blackwater Lake and, more specifically, since she'd met Cabot. But at first it had hurt. The humiliation was no fun, either. And she was a grown-up. Ty was a little boy. "Are you ever going to tell him?"

"If he wants to know."

"That seems wise," she agreed.

"You're judging again." This time there was a smile in his voice.

"In a good way."

"It's not wise. Just common sense," he claimed. "If you tell a kid he can't do something, that's exactly what he wants to do."

"Is that the voice of experience talking?" she teased.

"Maybe. Maybe not. I think of it more as human nature."

They had come full circle, past his house. She'd expected he would go inside and let her see herself back, but he didn't. Cabot walked her to her front door and stopped.

"Good night, Kate. Two more days until the kids get here. Get some rest. You're going to need it."

"See you," she said.

She watched him turn and walk back up the hill, a solitary man in the dark. Walking with him had been both exhilarating and enlightening. He had been married but was now divorced. She'd wanted so badly to say that he and his son were better off without a shallow, selfish woman like that having any influence on their lives. Only an idiot would run away from the child she'd borne and a man who loved her.

It was the running part that gave Kate pause. *She'd* run. Granted, the guy she'd left might be a good match for Cab's ex—in the shallow-and-selfish department. But still, she'd run. Did he put her in the same category as his ex-wife?

The thought troubled her, which was both annoying and not very bright. She'd just escaped from complications with a man and shouldn't let herself lose sleep over what this man thought. They'd only just met.

And she hoped to be wrong but couldn't shake the feeling that he might be pining for the woman who'd left him.

* * *

On the first day of camp Kate helped the other four counselors greet and sign in the kids, then assign cabins and settle them there. The other employees were all first-or second-year schoolteachers and this was their summer job. She was the only oddball without training.

It was late afternoon when she walked into the camp kitchen. The dining room was a log-cabin-style building, and the food-preparation area was situated behind the larger room where picnic tables would seat the campers for meals. A patio jutted off, and if they wanted, the kids could eat out there with a spectacular view of the lake. Without children around, it could be the perfect spot for a romantic dinner if you were with a man who looked like Cabot Dixon, one who might lean toward a little romance after a walk under the stars. He didn't seem to lean that way, but maybe she just wasn't his type.

And the fact that she would even wonder about this meant she probably needed serious therapy.

"Hi, Caroline." She greeted the manager/cook who was cutting up vegetables on the long stainless-steel counter in the center of the room. A six-burner stove stood behind her, and different-sized pots hung from a rack suspended from the ceiling.

The tall blonde looked up and smiled. "Did the kids scare you off?"

"No." But Kate grinned at the teasing. "They're a terrific bunch and I really enjoyed meeting them. But Jim told me to take a break while they divide the campers into color groups for activities."

"Jim Shields is a good teacher and really terrific at what he does here."

Kate knew Caroline worked with him at Blackwater Lake High School, where he taught math and was the boys' volleyball coach. "I came to see if you need any help in the kitchen."

"You don't want to put your feet up? Catch a power nap?"

"Working with children might not be my best skill, but I can take it. I'm sturdier than I look."

"What *is* your best skill?" the other woman asked.

Kate couldn't blame her for being curious. She'd shown up in a wedding dress and given no other information about herself besides the fact that she'd left her cheating weasel of a groom at the altar. But this peace and quiet felt good after so many years of nonstop media interest and craziness. It would end if the details about her came out. She wanted serenity for just a little bit longer.

"If you don't mind, I'd rather not say."

"Suit yourself." Caroline put down the knife in her hand. "I can use some help. Hamburgers and fries are the traditional first-night meal here, and I insist on fresh, not frozen, potatoes. You can cut them up. Real thin."

"Okay."

"When you finish that, would you slice some carrot and celery sticks? I always like to have those available."

"Got it."

Kate saw that the potatoes were already peeled and soaking in a pot of water. She got to work, and after checking the thinness of her fries, Caroline said nothing for a few moments. Finally Kate couldn't stand the silence. It was against all the laws of nature for two women to be in a kitchen together and not talk. Usually about men. And she knew exactly which man she wanted to talk about.

"How long have you managed the camp for Cabot?"

"Ten years now."

Tyler was eight, which meant this woman had met his mother. After the little bit Cabot had said, Kate had a lot of questions. "So what was Cabot's wife like?"

Caroline glanced up quickly from the tomato she was slicing. "Why do you want to know?"

"He told me what happened and why."

"Interesting." She looked up again. "He doesn't usually talk about it."

Should she feel special that he'd told her the story? A question for another day. "I guess I'm just curious what you thought of her."

"It's hard to answer that. There is my impression when he was first with her and my feelings about what she did to him by running away." She sighed and rested her wrist against the cutting board. "She was a very pretty little thing. Long black hair and violet-colored eyes. Seemed sweet and head over heels for Cabot. No one saw that she was unhappy or that she would do what she did. Folks were shocked, and some blamed it on postpartum depression. But she never came back to set things right. Cabot was stunned and dazed. The thing is, he didn't really even have time to process his feelings because he had an infant to care for and a business to run. Maybe that was a blessing."

Kate remembered his wistful tone when he'd talked about his wife. "Do you know how he feels about her now?"

"No," Caroline said. "As far as I know, no one knows."

Kate had been hoping for something specific, a tidbit to explain why he hadn't shown the least bit of interest in kissing her. It wasn't that she'd wanted him to get romantic, because that would complicate her peace and quiet. But she kind of wanted him to want to and be fighting it just a little. Crazy. Except that she was still feeling the effects of her fiancé cheating on her and the lingering questions about why she was found lacking. Maybe her self-confidence had taken a bigger hit than she'd realized.

"Does he have a girlfriend?" That would explain the lack of interest.

"Not that I'm aware of. And this is a small town," Caroline said pointedly. "If he did, everyone would know."

"He must have needs."

Caroline gave her a sharp look. "You're awfully curious."

"I'm sorry. That was really nosy. I didn't

mean to be inappropriate. But he's an exceptionally good-looking man. It's hard to believe he's been unattached for so long."

Kate figured if he had an itch that wasn't getting scratched and he'd still not been tempted by her, that would make her feel even more pathetic.

The other woman nodded, apparently understanding the curiosity. "Cabot likes women, if that's what you're asking. No one knows for sure, but the assumption is that he 'dates' discreetly. The last thing he'd want is talk linking him to anyone getting back to his boy. He'd never put up with that."

"Anyone can see he cares about Ty," Kate agreed. "He seems like a wonderful father."

"And then some." Caroline looked thoughtful. "Because of what happened, he's got a deep empathy for wounded people and goes out of his way to protect them."

That actually was a segue into something else she was curious about. "I have another question."

"I bet you do."

"Clearly I have no right and I'd like to believe it's not prying. Maybe inquisitive—"

"You think?" She saw humor in Caroline's blue eyes.

"Yeah. But I can't help it. I'm curious about the cabin where I'm staying."

"Why?"

"It was empty and available. Stocked with basics—including coffee and toiletries, like a hotel room. As if it was ready. Like people in areas that are prone to natural disaster keep emergency supplies up to date."

"*Natural disaster* and *emergency* pretty much describe Cabot's reasons for keeping it prepared."

"I don't understand."

"Folks call it the 'stray cabin.' Cabot has a soft spot for the three-legged dog or a blind cat. People, too. He keeps that place for anyone who's in need. Like the soldier returning from the war who needs quiet to deal with post-traumatic stress disorder. Or the homeless guy who lost his job and just needs a temporary place to stay while he gets back on his feet. Then there was the abused woman who left her husband, and Cabot made sure she was safe until the crisis was over."

"Very noble of him."

"Also, there's the occasional runaway bride," Caroline added drily.

"Not that I don't think he's an incredibly decent man, or that I'm ungrateful for his help, but I'm not a charity case," Kate assured her.

"Okay."

The tone was on the patronizing side and Kate felt obligated to share just a few big details. "In some circles I'm fairly well-known."

"That doesn't mean you don't need a little help."

"Not really," Kate assured her. "I can take care of myself. In fact, it will be news when I surface and I'll have to make a statement."

"You mean running out on your wedding wasn't statement enough?" Caroline asked.

"You know why I did it. And there are lots of reasons for running. That doesn't make me like his ex-wife."

"If you say so."

"I do." She winced at the words that she would have said if she hadn't run out on the wedding.

Kate would love to know what Cabot had said to this woman about her. If she had to guess, there was some comparison between her and the woman who'd done him wrong. Some judgment that lumped her in the same, unsympathetic group of females who were selfish and irresponsible.

"Look, Caroline, I did run out on my wed-

With school out, Ty was participating in camp activities. Caroline had explained this was child care for him so that his father could work. The boy had joined in on some of the events and had hung back on others. Swimming was his strongest skill; he was like a fish. He was not a shining star at basketball, football or baseball, and his lack of confidence showed in his facial expressions and body language. Tyler Dixon simply tugged at her heart.

It was now late afternoon. Everyone was taking a little breather before dinner. She'd checked with Caroline to make sure no help was needed for the evening meal. After getting the all clear, she'd decided to take a walk by the lake.

Even though she saw it every day, the beauty of Blackwater Lake still astounded her. It would never happen in a million years, but she wondered whether or not she would take the view for granted if she lived here.

She stopped at an outcropping of rocks at the water's edge, breathed in the pine-and flower-scented air and watched the sunlight turn the gently moving surface of the lake into a sparkling blue carpet. If not for her pesky attraction to Cabot Dixon, her soul would be at peace for probably the first time ever.

She hadn't talked to him for a couple of days, since that night he'd explained he walked ranch inspection every night. From the window of her tiny cabin she'd seen him pass by, but he didn't look over, obviously not even tempted to drop in and see her. She wasn't accustomed to serenity, but she also wasn't used to being ignored. Or being considered a "stray." It had been so hectic she hadn't had time to process what Caroline had told her about the cabin being available to Cabot's charity cases. She wasn't a three-legged dog or blind cat. Or an abused woman. It rankled some that he'd pegged her that way.

"As a rule a man's a fool. When it's hot he wants it cool. When it's cool he wants it hot. Always wanting what is not." She shook her head at the silliness of the ode to human nature that her mother had taught her.

"Kate—"

She whirled around, startled because she hadn't heard footsteps behind her. Ty stood there. "Hi. Wow, you were really quiet."

"You weren't." His freckled face was solemn. "Do you have an imaginary friend?"

"No. I was just talking to myself." She studied him. "Do *you?*"

"I used to. Then C. J. Beck—I mean, Stone—and me got to be best friends."

She was no shrink, but it wasn't much of a stretch to assume that this little boy was lonely. His father was busy running a business and his mother was somewhere in Montana but made no effort to see her son. No two ways about it. The situation just totally sucked.

"Do you want to walk back with me?" she asked.

He looked up hopefully. "Would it be okay?"

"I'd like that very much." She pointed to the way she'd come. "It'll be time for dinner pretty soon."

Ty fell into step beside her. "Can you have dinner with me and my dad again?"

"I'd like that," she said cautiously. "But you'd have to ask your dad if it's okay first."

He kicked a rock on the lakeshore. "I just know he'll say no."

Kate figured the only reason Cabot had allowed her to dinner that one time was because she'd just pushed ahead and didn't give him a tactful out. "Does your friend C.J. come to dinner?"

The boy thought for a minute. "Not very often. I usually go to his house."

"I'm sure your dad has his reasons."

"He works all the time," Ty agreed. "And C.J. has a mom and dad now. When there's school I go to his house a lot and either his mom or dad brings me home."

"That's nice."

"Yeah." He picked up a rock and threw it into the lake. "He got adopted."

"Oh?" Did C.J. have different biological parents? Her response was designed to elicit more information if Ty wanted to tell her.

"Yeah. Dr. Stone—Adam—got married to his mom and then adopted him."

"I see. Does he like Adam?"

"Yeah. But he calls him Dad now."

"That's really nice." She looked down, and it was impossible to overlook the brooding expression and longing on the small face.

"He's got a mom and dad."

"Do you miss your mom?"

He thought about that. "I was a baby, so I don't remember her."

If she read between the lines, he was saying you couldn't miss what you never had.

But you could certainly envy what someone else had. "I always had a mom and dad around, so I don't really know what you're going through. Guess it's hard to only have one parent, huh?"

"Most of the kids at school have two parents," he said. "I wish my dad would get married so I'd have a mom."

Uh-oh. She was afraid there was an ulterior, matchmaking motive to another dinner with them. Oh, God, what to do? She didn't want to reject him, but wasn't it more cruel to let him hope that she and his father would ever become romantically involved?

"Ty, are you hinting about me and your dad getting—close?"

He looked up. "Maybe. I think he likes you."

Kate wasn't so sure about that. "Why do you say that?"

He shrugged. "Prob'ly 'cause he looks at you funny."

Prob'ly he did that 'cause he wished he'd never laid eyes on her or offered her the "stray" cabin, she thought. "I'm flattered that you believe he's attracted to me. But you know it takes two people to like each other for anyone to even think about marriage."

"Yeah, I know." He kicked a well-worn

sneaker into the wet dirt at the lake's edge. "Do you like my dad?"

She'd walked right into that one. No way could she answer honestly, that she thought Cabot Dixon was the hottest cowboy she'd ever seen and one look into that handsome face made her heart beat way too fast. But there were too many stumbling blocks. He needed someone who would love the ranch and stay there. She thought it was the most beautiful place she'd ever seen, but she had to go back to her regularly scheduled life and numerous commitments. Letting this child go on hoping for a relationship felt heartless, and she couldn't let him continue.

She put a hand on his shoulder. "Ty, your dad is a great guy. He's a wonderful father and works very hard to take care of the ranch and you. But—"

"What? You like him."

"I do. But my stay here is temporary and you're talking about forever."

"Do you have to go?" His voice was wistful.

"Yes. I'm just taking a break here." She squeezed his thin shoulder. "Do you understand?"

"Yeah."

The tone said quite clearly that he didn't like it, though.

They were just passing the archery range, an open field where targets were secured on bales of hay. In the summer-camp compound, bows and arrows were stored in an equipment shed. Kate had dabbled in the sport because almost every shooting range where she practiced hitting clay targets also had an archery section. And she'd become friendly with some of the members of the Olympic team. Her roommate had come close to a gold medal but had to settle for silver. Today Kate had given some of the kids pointers to improve their form and accuracy. It had felt good to make a difference.

Ty glanced over at the field and frowned. "I'm no good at that."

"It's a difficult skill to learn and takes a lot of practice to master it."

"Dustin and Maddie are really good."

"They're older and have been to camp for the past several years," she said. One of the other counselors had filled her in on them.

"I'll never be as good as them."

Kate looked down at the boy's expression and recognized it from looking in the mirror twenty years ago. Because of all the moves her family made, she used to be him, on the outside looking in. The loneliness was consuming. Her parents had noticed and that was when her father started including her on his outings to the skeet-shooting complex. She'd wanted to try it and then amazed everyone with her raw ability. The rest was history.

But her parents were a team. Cabot was a single father and couldn't be faulted for not noticing his son's isolation. She suspected Ty wouldn't say anything because on some level he knew his dad was juggling so many things and didn't want to be a burden. Or risk that another parent would think he was too much trouble.

Unlike her, he was growing up in the place where he'd been born, but he still battled loneliness. This boy got to her, and suddenly the words were coming out of her mouth. "I could help you with archery. Privately."

"Really?" Excitement shone in his eyes when his gaze jumped to hers.

"I'd be happy to. Although you should know it's not my best event."

"Horseback riding is my best event," he said, clearly engaged now.

"Good for you. I'm afraid of horses."

"Really? They're easy compared to archery," he said, more carefree and a little cocky now. "I could help you get over it."

"I bet you could." And it would boost his self-confidence. "Let's make a deal. I'll teach you about archery and you help me with horses."

Tyler took the hand she held out and said, "Deal."

Would Cabot's average charity case be able to do that?

Cabot made sure Ty was sound asleep before starting his nightly inspection of the ranch buildings. It hadn't taken his son long to be out like a light; camp activities kept him busy and wore him out. Caroline had texted him that everything was fine before she went home for the day. As he walked down the hill all seemed quiet.

The program was a good one because he hired the best people to run it. His son was busy in a positive way and well supervised during the summer off from school. That meant Cabot could take care of business without worrying about him getting into trouble.

Earlier Ty had come in happy and excited after having dinner with the campers and said this year he was going to learn how to shoot a bow and arrow really good. That was a direct quote. And Kate was going to teach him. Why the heck would she know how? Maybe she'd had a class in college, but that would have been a while ago. Just showed Cabot how little he knew about the runaway bride.

He walked past the camp cabins, where he could see dim lights and hear quiet talking from inside. The crickets were louder than the kids, which told him the situation was normal. Moving on, he passed the cabin where Kate was staying and felt the same knot in his gut that he had every night when he forced himself not to look over and see if she was on the porch.

If he did and she was, the temptation to talk to her could be too much to resist. And if he didn't resist, there was a better-than-even chance he would make a move on that spectacular mouth of hers and live to regret it.

No, ignoring her was the smartest play and that was what he did.

Cabot came to the end of the dirt path, where a patch of grass bordered the lake. The moon was nearly full tonight, and he spotted a lone, slender female figure at the water's edge. Because the counselors were with kids and Caroline had gone home, he knew whom that body silhouetted against the moonlight belonged to.

Kate Scott.

Fate was putting another temptation in his path, but her back was to him. She didn't know he was there, which meant slipping away quietly was an option. He started to turn and his boot scraped a rock, a small sound that echoed loudly in the quiet night.

She looked over her shoulder. "Cabot?"

So much for slipping away quietly.

"Evening, Kate." He walked across the grass to stand beside her.

The sun had gone down. How was it possible that her lips looked even more appealing? Moonlight was sneaky that way.

"You're on routine inspection?" No greeting and her tone was cool, clipped, as if there was a chip on her shoulder about something.

"Yeah. Everything's quiet."

"No three-legged dogs creating havoc or blind cats bumping into trees?"

"Not that I've seen." Definitely a chip on her shoulder, and he had no idea what was on her mind.

"That's a relief."

He wasn't going to bite. Staying neutral and unengaged. "Nice night."

"Beautiful," she said, glancing up at the stars. "The sky is like diamonds on black velvet."

He followed her gaze. "Never thought about it like that, but could be."

"Tell me something."

"Okay," he said, bracing himself.

"I can't imagine ever taking all of this for granted. But I can't help wondering. Does it ever get old?"

"What? The scenery?"

"It's not just scenery. The lake. The mountains. Trees and flowers. Meadows. Everything."

"It never gets old, but I guess you get used to it. Every once in a while it's good to have a reminder of what's around you. See it all through someone else's eyes."

"That's what I figured."

Why did he have the feeling that he'd somehow let her down? And why should it matter if he did? He could see that she was brooding, and this time he couldn't stop himself.

"You okay?"

"Peachy."

Yeah, he could tell. But if she didn't want to talk about it… "Ty tells me you're going to give him pointers on using the bow and arrow."

"Yes. We have a bargain."

"Oh?" He couldn't wait to hear the terms of this deal.

"I'm going to work with him to improve his archery skills and he's going to teach me about horses."

There was a clue about her. "So, you've never been around horses?"

"No." Eyes narrowed, she met his gaze. "Do you have a problem with that?"

"Why should I? Lots of people don't know the first thing about horses."

"That's not what I meant and you know it." She huffed out a breath. "I was talking about the bargain with your son. Do you mind if I work with Ty? It seems important to him."

"I have no objection." He paused a moment, then said, "Where did you pick up archery skills?"

She stared at him for several moments, looking injured and insulted at the same time. For the life of him, he couldn't figure out what he'd done to tick her off.

Finally she said, "I'm not who you think I am."

"And who do you think I think you are?"

"A stray."

The light was beginning to dawn. "So you heard you're in what everyone calls the 'stray cabin.'"

"Yes. And it has to be said that I'm not some down-on-her-luck loser. Unless you're talking about my choice in men."

"Okay. But from my perspective, you showed up in a wedding dress, driving a truck that's seen better days and jumped at that Help Wanted sign in the diner window. Seems like a no-brainer that you needed a job."

"You ever heard the saying about judging a book by its cover?" She faced him squarely, hands on hips, agitation making her eyes shine and a muscle jerk in her delicate jaw.

His fingers itched to cup her cheek in his hand, turn her face up to his and smooth out the tension in her jaw. He'd known talking to her was a bad idea, and there was no satisfaction in being right.

"Yeah. I've heard the saying. And I'll take your word for it that what you're telling me is true." He started to turn away. "Night, Kate."

"Just a minute. I'm not finished." She put a hand on his arm to stop him.

Cabot felt the heat of her fingers clear

through to his gut. It got his attention in all the wrong ways and all the right places. "Okay. What else have you got?"

"I jumped at this job because I needed a time-out from my life. I wanted time to process what happened. How things went so badly. Get my head on straight and be able to do that in private."

They were standing so close that he could feel the heat of her body and smell the sweet floral scent of her skin. The combination smoldered inside him and he wanted to *feel* her everywhere. He needed to get away *now.*

"All right, Kate. If you say that's all there is to it, then I'll go with that."

Again he started to turn away and she stopped him. "I get that you have no proof what I'm saying is the truth. It's just words. So, donate my paycheck to the three-legged dog of your choice. Better yet, give it to your favorite charity. Wait—I know." She pointed at him. "Build another stray cabin with it. Makes no difference to me."

Cabot's willpower had been forged through crisis and disaster. In the years since his wife had walked out, he'd learned when to take someone on and when to walk away. It was all about survival. And right now his head was telling him to hit the road as fast as he could. The problem was other parts of him were telling him something else.

His self-control couldn't stand up to the force that was Kate. It felt as if he would burn up and blow away if he didn't kiss her. So he did the only thing he could.

He pulled her against him and lowered his mouth to hers.

Chapter Five

Kate tasted surprise and irritation on his lips and completely understood what he was feeling. It went double for her, along with the perversely conflicted inclination to stay like this for a good long time.

Then the full effect of it hit her like a meteor suddenly slamming into Earth. She'd never expected to feel that kind of power just from kissing a man. His mouth was soft and warm, chasing away the mild coolness of the beautiful summer evening. He brushed his fingers over her neck, scattering tingles through her body like sparks from a campfire and just as potentially dangerous.

Telling him to stop never crossed her mind. She realized that from the first moment she'd seen him, this was what she'd been hoping for. And maybe, just maybe, this was what it felt like to be swept away.

She slid her hands over his solid chest, linked her wrists around his neck and toyed with his hair. Maybe that was some kind of a signal because he traced the seam of her lips with his tongue, and when she opened for him, he entered her. He explored and caressed the sensitive interior of her mouth, making her want to feel his touch everywhere.

Her breasts pressed against his chest and seemed to swell in anticipation of more intimate pleasure to come. Raising on tiptoe to meet his mouth more firmly, she couldn't seem to get close enough. The sound of his harsh breathing combined with hers and drowned out the chirping crickets.

He kissed her mouth, her neck, her cheek and gently nipped her earlobe, sending more tingles zinging over her arms and down her spine. Her pulse raced and her blood simmered and sizzled in her veins.

His mouth began the sensuous task of reversing the path he'd just blazed when childish laughter echoed from one of the nearby cabins. Cabot froze for several seconds, then moved his lips away from hers.

"Damn—" His voice was ragged and full of self-censure.

"What?" she managed to ask. "Is something wrong? I don't get—"

He dropped his hands from her waist and stepped back, giving the night air space to come between their bodies and cool the heat they'd just generated. "This was a bad idea."

Define "bad idea," Kate thought. She'd only recently refused to go through with her wedding. But fighting the moonlight was more than she could manage. She was breathless from the feel of his mouth. Most of all she was deeply missing his body so close to hers and the feel of his lips taking her somewhere she'd never been before.

Bad idea? The words finally penetrated the sensuous haze fogging up her head and she wanted clarification. "What do you mean it was a bad idea?"

"This is all my fault. I take full responsibility."

He was making it sound as if kissing her was wrong. It sure hadn't felt wrong to her.

"I agree that you started it," she said. "But if a line was crossed, I think a case could be made for sharing accountability equally. But I'm not seeing the problem here."

"I wish I wasn't seeing it," he muttered.

"So, enlighten me."

Cabot dragged his fingers through his hair and she felt a great deal of satisfaction in the fact that his hand was shaking. "For starters, two weeks ago you ran out on your wedding."

"Yeah." That had just crossed her mind, too. And something else. She'd never felt like this when "the jerk" had kissed her. Proof that she'd never been in love with him. And, although she didn't really want to focus on this aspect right now, it was also proof that her judgment in men was questionable. "What's your point?"

"When a woman tells you she's taking a time-out, a break to get her head on straight, it crosses a *bad* line to kiss her. That wasn't smart of me."

She disagreed, and every sensually deprived nerve ending in her body was protesting, too. In spite of the intensity tightening his features, or maybe because of it, she felt compelled to argue.

"Sometimes a kiss has nothing to do with IQ or rational thought and everything to do with pure instinct."

"I'm not going to do this with you. Nothing good can come of debating the pros and cons of what just happened. And I say that because there's something more important going on here."

Admittedly her thought-processing mechanism was scrambled at the moment, but she couldn't think of anything that trumped chemistry and attraction. "I'll bite. Why are we making a federal case out of this?"

He angled his head toward the cabins. "What if any of the kids wandered down here and saw us?"

"They're not supposed to do that without a counselor present."

"Right. And kids have never broken rules before." His tone dripped sarcasm. "Parents entrusted their children to me and it would be a violation of that trust if one of their kids came across me kissing one of the counselors. An employee," he added.

"I see where you're coming from," she admitted. "But witnessing a kiss between a man and woman who are both single would hardly scar a child for life. Although, darn it, you do have a point."

"I'm glad you understand because it's not a chance I'm willing to take." He moved another step away from her. "I'm sorry, Kate. As you said, I started it. My fault entirely. And I promise you that it will never happen again."

Maybe just one more time, she thought. An experiment to see whether or not she'd really been swept away or just treading water.

But he turned and walked back the way he'd come, and the sight of his retreating back proved the wisdom of "show, don't tell" when making a point. He could stand there and say until hell wouldn't have it that the kiss was wrong and would never happen again, but leaving her in the dust said loud and clear that he took that pledge seriously.

How much of his action was motivated by sense of duty? How much was provoked by his sense of violated trust because his wife had broken her word to stay? And how much was prompted by the reality that he might still be in love with her?

Kate would probably never know the answers to those questions because Cabot Dixon impressed her as the sort who would maintain his distance because he always kept his promises.

In a man, that was both a blessing and a curse. And that frustrated her.

* * *

This wasn't Kate's first time sitting around a campfire, but it had never been part of her job before. Tonight they were bidding farewell to the kids who were staying for only a week. Others would be with them for another seven days and some were staying all summer.

The circular fire pit was made up of well-charred cinder blocks from past send-offs. It was located in an open area away from trees, shrubs and structures and not far from the lake, which offered them a view of the moon shining on the water.

Gotta watch out for that moonlight, she reminded herself. It could make a person do crazy things, like kiss a cowboy.

Kate was relieved that she wasn't leaving the camp until the end of the summer. But for the boys and girls who were going home, she felt a little sad.

Adults and children would sit around the fire on logs permanently placed there along with folding chairs that could be moved around as needed. The group had finished a final meal of salad, sloppy joes and chips, then filed out of the dining room and down to the fire pit. Two little girls, blonde Emily and dark-haired Hannah, had moved beside her and each grabbed one of her hands.

Kate was surprised. She'd interacted with all the kids and was friendly but firm. No one had been clingy until now. Probably that was a sign they were sad to leave.

"Hey, Em. Hannah." She smiled at the girls, who were ten and eleven, respectively. "How was dinner?"

"Good," they both said.

"I can't wait for s'mores." Emily skipped along, always full of energy until lights-out.

Hannah, tiny for her age, moved her short legs as fast as she could to keep up. "I just want a toasted marshmallow. Gooey and sticky. The boys usually just let them catch on fire."

"Ew," Kate said. "That's like eating ashes."

"Oh, they don't eat them," Emily explained. "It's the only way they're allowed to play with fire."

"I guess that's the way boys are," Kate agreed.

But Cabot was a man, and she figured cowboys had a different way of playing with fire.

The moon overhead was a reminder of Cabot starting a fire inside her. She hadn't seen him since he'd kissed her by the lake;

the residual embers from that searing kiss refused to go out.

"I wish this wasn't my last night." Hannah's voice was wistful.

"Me, too. Next year I want to stay longer," her ponytailed friend agreed. "I'm going to miss you, Hannah."

"Where do you live?" They reached the fire-pit area, and Kate looked around for two seats together for the girls. "Close enough to visit?"

"No." Emily shook her head. "I live in Dallas and Hannah is from Seattle."

"That's too far for a sleepover," Kate admitted. "You could exchange email addresses and phone numbers and keep in touch."

"That's what we decided," Hannah told her. She pointed to an empty space on one of the logs. "Why don't you sit between us over there?"

"Maybe after s'mores," she said. "I have to be up and around to help anyone who might need it. You girls go ahead and sit. Save me a place if you can."

The fire was already a healthy blaze, snapping and popping, bathing the area in a golden glow as it kept the shadows at bay around the circle. A quick glance told her all the campers were gathered around, although she didn't see Tyler. She'd noticed during the week that he wasn't always there for meals with the other kids. He could come and go; his presence or absence likely was based on his father's work schedule.

Caroline had a cardboard box containing metal skewers, graham crackers, chocolate squares and marshmallows. She was going to supervise making s'mores and was probably packing a fire extinguisher for anyone who decided to play with fire. Kate and the other counselors were going to handle simple roasting.

She'd thought kids plus fire would equal chaos and had stressed about keeping the campers safe and happy. But the activity was completely organized. The counselors knew what they were doing. On the first day everyone had been divided into groups, and tonight the kids waited for their color to be called before taking a turn at roasting a marshmallow or putting together s'mores.

She assisted a boy in getting his marshmallow firmly on the skewer, then managed to convince him it was beautifully toasted before it went up in flames. S'mores she left to

Caroline and the other adults experienced in that process.

The last group was almost taken care of when she heard her name called. She turned and saw Ty running toward her.

He stopped, nearly out of breath, and said, "Hi."

"Hey. Where were you? I didn't see you at dinner and worried you wouldn't get a chance to say goodbye to the kids."

"Dad took me to town and we went to the Grizzly Bear Diner. I needed new shoes and this was the only time he could take me. Mine are too small." He looked down at the old, ratty sneakers. "But he wouldn't let me wear the new ones tonight."

"I don't blame him. It's pretty dusty out here."

He looked up, his big eyes full of childish innocence and wonder about why that mattered. "They're just gonna get dirty tomorrow."

She laughed and ruffled his hair. "I guess it's just a dad thing that he'd like them to stay new for at least twenty-four hours."

"Guess so."

"Don't you want a s'more?" she asked.

"Nah. I had a Grizzly Bear burger and I'm stuffed."

"Maybe later," she suggested.

After everyone who wanted a s'more had been taken care of, Hannah and Emily ran over to her and grabbed her hands with their still-sticky fingers. Their freckled faces were streaked with chocolate. "Come sit with us now," they both pleaded.

She looked at the little boy. "Let's make room for Ty."

"Okay." Hannah grabbed his hand. "Come on."

So the four of them sat together on the log and somehow Ty ended up next to her on one side, with Emily on the other. Hannah sat beside the little boy. When they were settled, Kate glanced up and saw Cabot on the other side of the pit watching her. Just like that it wasn't the fire making her warm, but more memories of the man who'd held her close.

That night had been chilly and clear, just like it was now. But with the fire throwing so much light, the stars were hard to see, unlike when she'd been in Cabot's arms. That setting couldn't have been more romantic if it had been created for a Hollywood movie.

Her pulse was hammering now just like it

had then. Her breasts tingled, remembering the feeling of being held close and tight to his wide chest. It was disconcerting to realize she'd never reacted so strongly to a man's kiss before. And the glaring intensity in his expression right now was a clue that he'd felt something, too, and wasn't any happier about it than she was.

"Okay, kids, it's time for awards." Jim Shields, the tall, good-looking chief counselor, was standing by the pit in the center of the area. "First is Red Group, the overall winner of the Color War."

The kids in that group cheered and high-fived, then lined up to receive a ribbon.

"Greens, you came in first for water sports."

Another round of applause went up as the children got in line to receive their first-place prizes.

"Next is yellow for arts and crafts. This is probably the most artistically talented group of campers I've ever had the pleasure of working with."

Everyone clapped and cheered the artistic accomplishments of the yellow group. They were a little quieter than the others but no less pleased. Kate realized that no child would leave camp without an acknowledgment of their skill and participation in whatever activity they'd chosen. No one would be made to feel insecure or less than anyone else.

"Last, but certainly not least, we have the blues. And it's not about being sad that you're going home tomorrow." That got a laugh. "This group has excelled in animal care. The horses, cows, goats, lambs, dogs and cats are really going to miss you guys. Come on up."

After the children had taken their ribbons and found a seat again, Jim looked around at everyone sitting on the logs or in chairs. "This year we decided to give out a new and special award for our newest counselor. Kate, come on up."

She wasn't unaccustomed to being in the spotlight or under public pressure, but not with a man looking on whom she'd kissed in the moonlight a couple of nights ago. It didn't help that this man was also her boss.

She shook her head, trying to decline, but someone who might have been Caroline started a chant. "Kate! Kate! Kate!"

Sighing, she stood and walked over to the chief counselor. "I don't deserve an award."

"Wait until you hear what it is." He grinned, then looked out at the gathering. "Kate takes first place in the klutziest-counselor category.

For tripping over the soccer ball instead of kicking it."

Her knees were still skinned from that humiliating episode. "Not my finest hour."

"Also for trying to do a header at soccer practice and almost knocking herself out."

"Soccer is not my best sport," she admitted.

"Neither is basketball—" Laughing and hooting erupted as the kids called out teasing comments. "Enough said on that."

"No one is perfect."

"This award is also for being a good sport about it all. And doing your best even though it wasn't pretty."

"Thanks." She took her ribbon, and for some reason her gaze drifted to Cabot.

His mouth was pulled tight and hard, but she remembered his lips being soft and arousing. He was either recalling their kiss or planning on terminating her employment for lack of ball skills. At least she was good for the kids' self-esteem. She'd made them all look good because she was so bad.

When she went back to her seat, Emily and Ty made room for her. She noticed that the ribbon said Number One Goofball and she laughed. Her Olympic teammates would think this was hilarious.

"My parents would be so proud," she said.

"Really?" Ty looked up at her, eyes wide.

"They'd think it's funny. I do, too," she told him.

"I'm not sure what my dad would think." He glanced over at the man on the other side of the circle, standing a little off to himself.

"I think all you have to do is your best and he'll be proud of you." Right now all he looked was wary.

"I'm not so sure," Ty said.

"Why do you say that?"

The small shoulders lifted in a shrug. "I guess maybe I'm not doing my best at some stuff."

"Like what?" she asked.

"Well..." He thought for a moment. "He tells me not to mope when the kids leave every week. That some stay on for a little longer, but sooner or later they all have to go. And I try not to be sad, but I guess I can't help it."

"I suppose it's pretty hard not to be," she said, giving him a quick hug. "But did you ever think about the fact that when you're sad, that makes your dad feel bad?"

"I guess I never did think about that." He

looked thoughtful. "But I like it when all the kids come in the summer."

"It's great for them, too. A chance to see what it's like to live on a ranch." She tapped his nose gently. "And there's stuff to keep you busy while you're out of school and your dad is working and can't spend time with you."

"Yeah." He nodded.

"The experience is sort of like life," she said. "People come into our lives for a short time and we learn that we'll go on and be fine without them."

"Kind of like what happened with my mom."

"Exactly." When Kate answered, she forced a cheerful note into her voice that was the opposite of what she felt.

She could have smacked herself for reminding him about that. When she looked over at Cabot, he was still watching—and frowning. It dawned on her that this reaction could be about his son seeking her out and sitting by her. Talking to her.

He was standing guard over his child. And good for him. Cabot knew she wasn't staying after the summer any more than these campers were, and he was afraid Ty was getting attached to her. She wouldn't like and respect him nearly so much if he didn't give a flying fig about his son.

She sympathized with Cabot and his concerns. If anyone knew how it felt to make friends and then lose them, it was her. And she'd had to learn to work it out. That was part of growing up.

But it didn't feel right to push this vulnerable little boy away. Plus, she'd made a deal with him to work at improving his skills with a bow and arrow. Cabot wasn't the only one who took promises seriously. That meant spending a little more time with him than she normally would.

All she could do was try to protect this boy, too. Remind him that when summer was over, like the kids who came to camp, she would be leaving, too.

She had a life waiting for her and it wasn't here.

Chapter Six

No matter how hard he tried, Cabot just could not get the picture of his son talking to Kate out of his mind because the two of them made a really nice picture. She seemed good with Ty—and he clearly ate up the attention. The problem was Cabot knew how it felt when someone stole your heart, then left it behind. He didn't want the boy he loved more than life itself to hurt that badly at such a tender age.

Cabot wasn't stupid. He knew sooner or later the kid would get his feelings stomped on. It happened to everyone. But if it was up to him, that would happen later rather than sooner.

"This is the barn." Speaking of the devil, he could hear Ty now.

It was late afternoon and Cabot was standing in the barn rubbing down his horse after a long workday. The jet-black pony was tired and hungry and Cab knew just how he felt. He'd take Ty up to the house for dinner and some quality father-son time. They didn't get enough of it.

"These are the stalls. Don't be scared," Ty said, coming into view where the gate was open wide.

And right behind him was Kate.

Cabot's pulse jumped at the sight of her and that was damned annoying. She was all tanned arms, big green eyes and sun-streaked brown hair. In her purple Camp Dixon T-shirt, ponytail and no makeup, she hardly looked older than the kids he paid her to supervise.

"Hi, Dad. I didn't know you were here."

"Hey, son." Would the kid have brought her here if he'd known? "I finished up early."

"Hello, Cabot." Kate stuck her hands in the pockets of her jeans. "I had a break and Ty offered to help me get over my fear of horses."

"It's not her best event, Dad."

"I see." Kind of an unusual way to phrase it, he thought.

But Cabot didn't put too much time into analyzing that. He was dealing with a fatherly pang over how grown-up the boy sounded—protective. The way a guy should be with women. His dad had drilled it into him that men were bigger and stronger. Along with that came a responsibility to look out for anyone smaller and weaker. He was trying to instill the lesson into his own son, and it looked as if the message was taking.

"I hope I'm not intruding," she said.

"Nope. This is a good time," he told her.

Ty moved into the stall beside the horse. "This is Blackie."

Kate's mouth quirked up at the corners. "I wonder why."

"Because he's black—" Ty saw her expression and grinned. "You were teasing."

"I definitely was," she confirmed.

Cabot continued to drag the stiff-bristled brush over the horse's flank. "This is a real good time to get acquainted. He's tired out from working all day. In the morning after a good night's sleep, he's frisky and full of energy. Not as quiet as he is now."

Kate was staying by the stall's opening, deliberately not moving closer. Apprehension darkened her eyes nearly to brown and tightened her mouth. “But he’d still be as big.”

“Blackie’s just a little guy,” Ty told her. “Dad likes to ride him on the line ’cause he’s fast and has quick moves if any of the cattle take it into their head to make a run for it.”

Cabot hid a smile at the way the boy repeated to her what he’d been told. Good to know he was actually listening when his old man said something. Sometimes he wondered. “It’s a cowboy’s job to be smarter than the animals, to anticipate their moves and be ready to counter.”

“Come over and touch him, Kate,” Ty urged. “Don’t be afraid. Blackie won’t hurt you.”

“He’s right,” Cabot told her. “This pony is as gentle and sweet as they come. I won’t let him get out of line with you.”

Ty met his father’s gaze, then looked at the woman hanging back, and a gleam stole into his dark eyes. “Dad, I just remembered something I forgot to do.”

Without further explanation, the boy turned and ran past Kate and out of the barn before Cabot could say “hold your horses.”

He glanced at where his son had disappeared, then at her. "I apologize for him. Can't imagine what that was all about."

"Really?" Amusement danced in Kate's eyes. "You don't know?"

"Do *you?*"

"I have a pretty good idea."

"Care to share?" he asked.

"Of course. It's something I suspected at the campfire the other night, but his behavior just now confirmed my suspicions."

"Of what?"

"Tyler wants a mom. Like his friend C. J. Stone."

"Technically," Cabot told her, "C.J.'s mom got married and gave him a dad."

"So he's told me." She leaned a shoulder against the fence, still keeping her distance. "The point is, he wants the parent he doesn't have in order to get a complete set. And he seems to have picked me."

"Well, that's not good," he muttered.

"I'm going to try not to take offense at that." She gave him a saucy look. "And it has to be said that I'm not completely without maternal skills."

"That's not what I meant. It came out wrong." He rested his hand on Blackie's back. "Let me rephrase."

"I get it. My job is for the summer only. I'm here temporarily," she said for him. "Believe it or not, I actually agree with you. It's not good. No one, especially me, wants that child to be disappointed or hurt when his expectations aren't met."

"Amen," he agreed.

"But I'm pretty sure when he saw you here, he decided to play matchmaker and leave us alone. Let nature take its course, so to speak."

Cabot remembered the last time they were alone. Nature had taken its course all right. He'd kissed her. Surprised the heck out of himself when he'd done it and no matchmaking had been required. He'd chalked it up to the heat of the moment when she'd been giving him a piece of her mind. But she wasn't telling him off right this minute and he still wanted to kiss her.

The light wasn't all that good here in the barn, but he would swear her cheeks turned pink. He'd also swear she was remembering that moonlit night, too. He'd managed to pull together his self-control and walk away, but thinking about her all the time was taking a toll.

"So, you're saying that he's trying to push us together?"

"I think so, yes." She nudged the hay with the toe of her sneaker, not quite meeting his gaze. "Far be it from me to give fatherly advice, Cabot, but I hate the thought of Ty being hurt. I'd talk to him myself about why things with us can't be the way he wants, but it would be better coming from you."

He appreciated her sensitivity to his son and found himself admiring her straightforward manner. No games. No pretense. Just state the problem and a solution. Practical and appropriate.

"I agree. And I'll have a chat with him to explain."

"Good. That makes me feel a lot better." She smiled at him as if he'd hung the moon.

Cabot felt the pull of that smile clear down in his gut. He had a finely honed mistrust of women in general and this one in particular. In spite of that, being with her was like enjoying the first day of spring after a long, cold winter.

"Don't worry about Ty. He's tough."

"He's a charmer, that's for sure. You've got a terrific kid there."

"I know." Giving him that boy was the only thing he was grateful to Ty's mother for.

Other than that, she'd left a trail of emotional destruction in her wake.

"Speaking of kids… I should get back."

Her body language said she was going to bolt, but Cab wanted to hang out in her sunshine just a little longer. So he said the only thing he could think of to get her riled. "Coward."

"I'm sorry?"

"You're going to cut and run without getting close to this horse?" Now for the challenge. "What would Ty say?"

"Probably that I'm a coward." She shrugged. "I'm okay with that."

"Blackie will feel rejected."

"I'm okay with that, too."

"I'm really disappointed in you, Kate." He pointed at her. "And don't tell me you're okay with that. This is a working ranch and some of the camp kids want to spend time with the animals. Consider it part of your job description."

Her mouth pulled tight and she glared in his general direction, then finally nodded. "Feel free to check the 'uncooperative' box on my employee evaluation."

He didn't say anything, just watched her

inch forward. Then she stopped, keeping him between her and the horse.

Cabot stepped aside. "If he wanted to, a horse can hurt you with his hooves and his teeth, so a side approach is pretty safe."

"Good to know."

"Just put your hand on his neck."

"What if he decides to bite?" She looked up at him nervously.

"He'd have to move his head and you'd have plenty of time to react," he assured her.

Her hand was shaking when she lifted it and he covered it with his own. Setting her palm on Blackie's long neck, he showed her how it was done.

"Just rub him, like you would a dog or cat."

"If he were that small, I wouldn't have a problem." But she didn't pull away as he gently moved her hand up and down the long neck.

"He's not really soft," she observed.

No, but *she* was, Cab thought. He'd settled his other hand at her waist and it took every ounce of his willpower not to explore the curves that were just inches away from his fingers.

"His coat is coarse." He heard the ragged

edge in his voice. Blackie nickered softly, as if he sensed the reaction.

"Is he okay?" Kate asked, tensing.

"Fine. Just his way of letting you know that he likes it." Cabot couldn't see her face, but he could still feel her tension. "You doing okay?"

"Yeah. This isn't so bad."

Just as she said that, Blackie threw his head back and shifted to the side. Startled, Kate let out a squeak that was not quite a scream, then turned as if to run. Cabot's arms automatically went around her, pulling her close. At least he told himself it was automatic. Then he shifted, putting himself between her and the horse.

"You're okay," he crooned. "That wasn't a predatory move. He was just shifting his weight to be more comfortable. Like we do when we're standing."

In a reclining position, he could think of a lot they could do. And the warmth of her body, the softness of her pressed against him and the scent of her skin made him want that more than his next breath.

Kate clutched at him. "I'm sorry. It's just that was unexpected."

"I know. Don't worry about it," he said easily. "You'll get comfortable after a while."

"Yeah." She blew out a breath and snuggled just a fraction closer. "I'm sure that's true."

The same thing could be said about the two of them, Cabot thought. Spending time together could make him drop his guard and that was all kinds of bad. He put his hands on her arms and set her away from him.

"You okay?" he asked.

"Fine. Feeling a little silly," she said, "but fine."

"Good."

He was feeling silly, too, but for different reasons. It was stupid, but he wanted to kiss her, in spite of the fact that she worked for him and he'd made a promise to her that it would never happen again. Didn't take him but a couple of days to nearly break his word, and that was a big black mark on his integrity.

Kate must have seen something in his expression because she said, "I'm not being a coward, but Caroline might need some help in the kitchen. It's really time I get back to the job."

"Right."

She backed up toward the stall's open gate. "Thanks for trying to help me with my large-animal phobia."

"No problem."

"See you, Cabot." She turned and walked away, taking the feminine floral scent with her.

It had been on the tip of his tongue to say he would help her anytime, but he stopped those words from coming out of his mouth. She was here at the ranch for a paycheck. And his job was to work harder at not making another mistake with her.

Kate took her dinner tray out to the patio overlooking Blackwater Lake. The dining room was loud with excited kids chattering about the day and banging plates and glasses while they did. It was a kid-friendly environment and that was appropriate. But it was also crowded and there weren't any seats left. Outside only two seats were available, and she took one of them.

These children were the quieter, more artistic ones, so it was less noisy here. Peacefully beautiful. A strange feeling came over her…contentment. She hadn't felt it for a long time; possibly she never had, given her nomadic childhood.

She looked at the redheaded girl beside her. "Hi, Amanda."

After a shy smile the child said, "Hi."

“Are you enjoying your dinner?” She directed the question to the four children at the table—two boys and two girls.

“Chicken nuggets are my favorite.” Dylan was a dark-haired, freckle-faced nine-year-old.

“Good.” Again she glanced around, trying to draw all of them out. “How do you feel about carrot sticks?”

“I’d rather have ice cream.” That was Ryder, a charming blond, blue-eyed heartbreaker in training.

“Me, too.” Kate laughed. “But veggies are important.”

“That’s what my mom says.” Lisa pushed her black-framed glasses up on her nose.

“Yeah, moms are like that.” She took in the lake, mountains and trees and breathed deeply. “Don’t you love it here?”

Before anyone could answer, the sound of two voices carried from the dining room behind her.

Caroline was saying, “It’s about time you joined us to see how your summer-camp program is working out.”

“I have good people running it for a reason. If there’s a problem they can’t handle, and by that I mean you, I'll hear about it." That deep voice definitely belonged to Cabot.

"That's a given. So what did we do to deserve a visit from you?"

"Just wanted to check on Tyler and see how he's doing with the other kids."

"And?" Caroline asked.

"He was so busy talking, he didn't even know I was there."

"That's the way it should be."

"I know."

"And now you're stuck eating dinner here." Caroline waited for a response.

"I wouldn't put it like that," he said.

"I would." Humor mixed with a dash of challenge was in the woman's voice. "Looks like the only seat left in the house is right there beside Kate. Enjoy your chicken nuggets."

"Thanks."

Kate held her breath and listened to the scuff of boots on the wooden deck as he approached. Then a shadow blocked out the light when he stopped beside her.

"I understand this seat isn't taken."

"It is now."

She looked up at him because it was the polite thing to do. With the waning sunlight behind him and the shadow of his black Stetson distorting his features, it was impossible to guess what was going through his mind. But his lips were pressed together and a muscle jerked in his jaw.

That was all it took to figure out that he wasn't happy about this forced proximity, either.

She slid over to make more room for him. "Kids, this is Mr. Dixon. He owns the ranch and the summer camp."

Then she introduced the four children by name and each of them said hello.

"Are you a cowboy?" Dylan asked.

"Yes."

"What do cowboys do?" Lisa wanted to know.

"Let's see..." He took a bite of one of the nuggets and chewed thoughtfully. "I help the other cowboys take care of cows. Make sure the herd stays together—it's safer for them that way. Move them somewhere else when the food supply is running out. Watch over the ones who are going to have babies and help if necessary."

"Is it hard?" Amanda's sky-blue eyes widened.

"Can be," he answered. "Animals need

looking after three-hundred-sixty-five days a year. They don't take the summer off or Christmas vacation."

"But you get to ride a horse." Dylan clearly thought that made it the best job in the world.

"His horse's name is Blackie," Kate informed them. "Because he's black. I got to touch him."

Just then Cabot's arm brushed hers and sparks resulted as surely as if flint and steel had rubbed together. Not more than two hours ago he had held her in the barn; steadying hands had pulled her against him.

Kate was sure he'd been about to kiss her… and then he hadn't. She'd wanted him to, and the warmth of his body beside hers right now rekindled the wanting. Just because this wasn't the time or place didn't mean she'd get over the feeling anytime soon.

Cabot was watching her. "You're not eating."

That was because she could hardly breathe, let alone bite, chew and swallow. "I guess I'm not all that hungry."

An awkward silence stretched between the two adults as the kids made observations about cows, horses and what they wanted to be as grown-ups. Kate found that not talking was worse than carrying on a conversation with him. Every time either of them shifted even a fraction of an inch, their bodies touched. In the absence of any distraction, the contact was magnified and the reaction compounded.

She had to say something. "So, I've been reading up on Montana plant life."

"Oh?" He looked at her.

"Yes. I thought the bearberry was interesting. At first I thought it was the politically correct name for a bear's—you know."

"Yeah. I get it." Surprise, surprise. He actually smiled at that.

"Turns out I was wrong. Not only is it edible either raw or cooked, but also Native Americans added it to venison or salmon. They also dried it into cake and ate that with salmon eggs."

"Sounds tasty." Amusement sparkled in his eyes.

"Apparently it isn't all that tasty, but it can be useful as an emergency food if chicken nuggets aren't available."

"Good to know if I'm stuck in the wilderness."

"Speaking of that..." She realized he wasn't making this talking thing easy. But she was nothing if not determined. “If one ever does get stuck, fire is probably the number one tool of survival.”

“I’m aware of that.”

“It’s useful to stay warm, cook food, sterilize if necessary and signal for help.” She figured he knew all of this but wanted to let him know she wasn’t without skills.

“That’s what matches are for.”

“What if they get wet?” she challenged. “Do you know nine ways to start a fire without them?”

“Do *you?*” Skepticism was written all over his face.

“Of course.” She held up a hand and started to tick off the ways. “Friction-based using a fire board and spindle. The wood you choose is important. Cottonwood, juniper and walnut are best. You make a hand drill. Build a tinder nest with dry grass or twigs, put a V-shaped notch in the board and insert a stick, then start spinning.” She held up another finger. “Flint and steel are obvious. Make sparks. Fire good.”

“That’s basic,” he commented.

“Then there’s the lens-based method.” She thought this next one would get his attention. “Every little boy has melted his plastic action figures this way. You can use a magnifying glass, binocular lens or eyeglasses and let the sun reflect through it until your tinder ignites."

"Again, basic."

"You can also use a balloon. Or a condom," she added, dropping her voice so the children present couldn't hear. They were still chattering among themselves.

"You're joking."

She held up her hand. "I swear."

"How?"

"Fill it up with water—not too full or it will distort the sunlight's focal point. Make it as spherical as possible. You want to create a sharp circle of light, then hold it an inch or two from the kindling. The other one, not the balloon," she said, making sure the kids weren't listening, "you can try squeezing in the middle to form two smaller lenses."

"Is this your normal, run-of-the-mill party talk?" He looked both impressed and uncomfortable.

At least he was now participating in the exchange. "Actually, it is." When you were the public face of an outdoor-equipment brand, a girl needed to know what she was talking about. "I've used all nine techniques with success."

"I'd like to see that." He shook his head and actually laughed.

Kate felt as triumphant as if she'd won a national championship. Not only that, she thought he was more carefree and incredibly handsome with a smile on his face. "You should do that more often."

"What?"

"Smile. Laugh. It looks good on you," she said.

Just like that the laughter disappeared. He looked uncomfortable, as if he'd somehow broken an unspoken rule. "I don't know what to say to that."

"It was just an observation." But she was incredibly sorry she'd said it out loud.

He stood up, as if he couldn't get away from her fast enough. "Speaking of observing, I'm going to see what Ty is up to."

"Right. Of course. That's why you came to dinner in the first place."

"See you." He picked up his hardly touched food and walked away.

Kate sat there, her head spinning at how quickly her casual words had changed his attitude. Was he not supposed to have fun? Was it somehow against his code of honor? Maybe this was about the woman who'd walked out on him, some misplaced loyalty to vows taken, even though she'd broken them first.

Or he still had feelings for the mother of his son.

It was as if he'd forgotten any of that for just a few minutes with her, and then after he'd violated his personal code of honor, he couldn't get away from her fast enough. Her feelings wanted to be hurt, but in reality it was just as well he'd left.

She was here for a break from men as much as she was from the rest of the chaos that was her life. It made absolutely no sense on any planet for her to get involved with a handsome cowboy she would walk away from when summer was over.

Chapter Seven

Just before lunch the next day, Ty asked Kate if it was a good time to work on archery. The other kids were busy with activities he'd chosen not to participate in. She carved out a half hour for him right then, partly because of her promise, but mostly because the vulnerability on his face tugged at her heart. She had no idea why Ty was so determined to improve his skill, but probably it had something to do with getting his father's attention to make him proud.

Hopefully Cabot had talked to the boy about the fact that she and his father would never be a couple. She and Ty were alone on the archery range, standing at a line about ten feet from a bale of hay fitted with a target. The boy had picked out the bow and a quiver of arrows from the equipment shed. It seemed to be the right size for him.

Kate stood at the line beside him. "The first thing you need to do is set your stance."

"Kind of like baseball when you're batting."

"If you say so." She smiled down at him. "It's pretty clear that I know very little about that sport. You could tell by the way I couldn't catch or throw the ball."

"You were kind of bad. Sorry," he said.

"Honesty is always best." She ruffled his hair. "If I wanted to and had time, practice would improve my baseball skills, although it will never be my best event."

"What is?"

Kate didn't want him to have information about her Olympic sport and share it with his father. It would be too easy for him to look her up on Google and find out that in some circles she was pretty recognizable. For now she wanted to be anonymous and enjoy the peace and quiet. Soon enough she would have to resume the craziness of her life but not yet.

Vagueness was the way to go with his question, followed closely by a distraction.

"Like archery, my best event involves a target." Of course, the ones she aimed at were moving and made of clay. "Some of my friends were very good at it and taught me the basics. So, like I said, the first thing is your stance." She positioned him facing the target, leaving no time for more questions about her sport. "Put your feet shoulder-width apart with your weight evenly distributed."

"Like this?"

She checked him out. "Looks good. Now move your left foot back about six inches."

"Okay."

She nodded approval. "Next step is to grip your bow with your thumb and index finger, then slide the notch of your arrow onto the bowstring. That's called 'nocking.'"

"Sounds weird." Ty looked up quizzically and squinted into the sun.

"It's just a fancy word for loading the arrow to point it at the target."

"Okay."

"Relax your fingers. The palm of your hand should never apply pressure. Think of it as hanging your bow on hooks on the wall and keeping it steady. Your other hand is going to do the hard work."

"Okay." He held it as instructed, then looked up. "Now what?"

"Lift your bow and point the arrow at the target. Keeping your hand as still as possible is the most important fundamental in shooting." Any kind of shooting, she thought.

When her father had first taken her shooting as a way to help her adjust after another move, he'd been surprised at how steady she was. And that had continued, but only in her event. Life was far less controllable.

An image of Cabot Dixon drifted into her mind along with the memory of sitting next to him at dinner last night. Her senses had soaked up the whole experience until he'd had the presence of mind to walk away.

"Kate?"

"Oh, sorry. Lost my concentration." *Steady as you go,* she reminded herself. She stood behind him and nudged his bow hand to align it with the target.

He tightened his fingers and the arrow fell off. Frustrated, he looked up and said, "That happens a lot."

"Because you're holding it too tightly. Relax." When he was ready again, she said,

"Raise the bow and draw back the string. Then find your anchor point."

"What's that?"

"It's the place on your face where the hand is placed consistently with the bowstring at full draw and is most comfortable for you."

"How will I know where that is?" he asked.

"Practice. For now, put it by your jaw and we'll see what happens. You're all lined up with the target. Just keep loose and release the arrow with your fingers. Try not to move any other part of your body."

He did as instructed and the arrow fell short of the target. His body language screamed discouragement. "That happens a lot, too."

"Try again," she urged.

He did and the same thing happened. Kate checked his stance and finger position, then helped him pull back the bowstring a little farther. She made sure his fingers were loose, then directed him to release. It hit the hay bale just below the mark.

"Better," she praised.

"I still didn't get a bull's-eye."

"That takes practice, kiddo. This sport is different from baseball, where speed comes from your shoulder and accuracy is in follow-through with your arm. Archery is about focus, steadiness and aim. And how you set yourself up. How far you pull back the bowstring gives your arrow oomph, and follow-through is best when you can hold your position toward the target."

Ty continued to practice, and she helped him make adjustments until one of his arrows hit the target's outer ring.

"Did you see that?" His face glowed with excitement.

She grinned at him. "Excellent shot."

"Wow, I'm better already, thanks to you. I can't wait to tell C.J."

"He'll be very impressed," she agreed.

"Maybe I can show *him* how to do it."

"That would be great and would help you, too. But your dad or another adult should supervise," she suggested.

"I know. That's what he always says." Ty took another shot, and the bowstring snapped against his tender inner arm. "Ow."

"Let me see." She went down on one knee to check him and saw a small red mark but nothing serious. "That happens a lot. If you want to practice a lot, there's a guard you can get to protect you and keep it from hurting." She could see that his arms were shaking. It was time to call it quits. "I think that's enough for today. Why don't you pick up all the arrows?"

"Okay." He did as asked and put them back in the quiver, then returned to where she stood. "Next time C.J. comes over, could you supervise us?"

"That's up to your dad and Caroline. I might have things to do for the camp kids."

"I'll ask them," he said. "C.J. likes coming to my house to get away from his baby sister."

Kate laughed and started walking back toward the cabins. "She's annoying?"

"He says she cries a lot and is stinky." He shrugged. "I think she's kinda cute, but I don't tell him that."

Not macho, she thought. "What's her name?"

"Sophia Marie."

"Pretty name."

"I guess." He slung the bow over his shoulder. "Seems to me it would be cool to have a sister or brother."

"It has pros and cons," she commented.

"Do you have a sister?"

She nodded. "And a brother."

"Do you like them?"

"Yes." Although she'd heard her brother was a little peeved at her for taking his truck in her wedding escape. Pointing out that he also had a luxury car apparently hadn't appeased him, according to her mother. She'd asked her mom to tell Zach that she promised he would have it back by Christmas so he could get a tree, which, as far as she could tell, was his only reason for hanging on to the thing. "But brothers can be annoying, too."

"Well, I'd like one. Or a sister."

It was hard to know what to say because she was pretty sure that his dad was not on board with that. "Kids are a lot of responsibility, and your dad has a lot going on with you and the ranch."

"Do you like babies?"

The question didn't come completely out of the blue because the conversation was headed in this direction. Like she'd said at the beginning of his lesson, honesty was always best. "Yes. I think babies are cute, although I haven't had much experience with them."

"Do you want one?" His expression was hopeful.

Again she had to tell the truth. "Someday. When I fall in love and get married."

Ty stopped and looked up. "Do you like my dad?"

Oh, kiddo, she wanted to say. *Please don't make me break your heart.* Obviously Cabot hadn't talked to him yet about not trying to get them together.

She went down on one knee so their gazes were almost level. "Ty, I do like your father, but not in that way."

But he got serious points for being a spectacular kisser.

"What way?"

"Well, he's my boss." She thought for a moment. "And I think we're friends." Probably. Although the attraction was confusing. "The thing is, you have to remember that I'm only going to be here for the summer. When camp is over, I'll be leaving."

"Do you have to?"

Her heart was twisting in her chest. As gently as possible, she said, "Yes."

"Then can you help me practice archery a little bit every day so I can get better?" he asked.

"That would be great. And this seems to be a good time for it. We'll call it a standing date—unless," she cautioned, "Caroline has something for me to do."

"Cool." He sighed. "I sure hope that before you have to go, I can make archery my best event."

And she hoped that when she went, leaving this boy didn't break her heart.

Wearing a slicker in the rain, Cabot walked from the house down to the camp building where meals were served. He could never decide if this weather was more miserable in the summer or winter. Either way it was nasty. Because of it he'd assigned to the hired help only the chores that couldn't be put off and then instructed them to get inside ASAP. He was on his way to get a status report on how the campers and counselors were handling being cooped up inside.

It was about three o'clock when he walked into the empty dining room. Looking out the sliding glass door to the patio, his gaze was automatically drawn to the picnic table where he'd sat beside Kate. A reluctant smile curved the corners of his mouth as he remembered her explaining how to start a fire with a condom. The smile disappeared when he realized that putting Kate, condoms and fire in the same thought was dangerous. The problem was that he was having a devil of a time getting her *out* of his thoughts.

"Damn it," he muttered.

He couldn't have just let her get back in

that beat-up old truck and keep on driving. Not him. The stray guru. He had to go and hire her.

Shaking his head, he walked past the steam table and stainless-steel counter where the kids lined up to fill their plates buffet style. Behind this room was the kitchen. In the back was a storeroom and small office, which was where he found Caroline now, working at the battered and scarred old desk. On top was a laptop computer, upright file holder and a coffee mug with the words *Camp Dixon* on it that held pens, pencils and a bright yellow highlighter.

He stood in the doorway. “Hey, Caroline.”

Dragging her gaze away from the computer screen, she looked up, reading glasses resting low on her nose. “Cabot, I hate this weather. And I’m pretty sure the camp counselors are hating it even more than I am.”

“Days like this make me wish my job was in an office.”

“Then you’d have to wear a suit and tie.” Blue eyes took his measure.

“Yup.” He almost never thought about what his life might have been like if he hadn’t been obligated to take over the ranch responsibilities. But on days like today… “Today it might be worth it. The rest of the time, probably not." He had begrudgingly taken over the ranch and was a single father to Tyler, but he was the boss and didn't have to ask anyone for permission to come and go. "Guess every job has its pros and cons."

"Yes, they do." As the rain pounded on the roof, she added, "We need to remember to be grateful for this drenching. Some parts of the country are in a terrible drought."

"True enough," he said.

He'd heard stories from his father and grandfather about hard times when the land was parched and grass for the cattle to graze on was scarce. Hopefully that wouldn't happen on his watch. Not that he could control it any more than he could control his damned attraction to Kate.

"Tomorrow when the sun is out, I'll be grateful. Today I really feel like complaining."

"Is the weather responsible for this mood?" Caroline removed her glasses and set them on the desk, topping a stack of file folders. "Or is it something else? Or *someone?*"

Whether or not that was the case, Cabot knew it was always best to let her say what was on her mind. "Why don't you share your theory about my disposition?"

"Clearly it's not PMS." Her tone was wry.

"Got that right." Probably things would be easier if that was his problem.

"Seriously, though, it seems to me that your grumpiness can be traced back to the day Kate arrived in town."

Cabot wasn't sure she was right about that, but he could put a finer point on the observation. He'd started to feel really jumpy after realizing Ty had ideas to push Kate his way. That wasn't going to happen; only bad could come of it. So far there hadn't been an opportunity to have a father-son chat about the situation, but he would make it happen soon.

"You're not completely wrong about that," he admitted.

The blonde leaned back in the chair as she studied him. "Do you like her?"

"What is this? High school?" He tried to make light of the question. "You've been hanging out with teenagers too long."

"Maybe. But unlike some people I could name, I'm not living under a rock. *And* I don't deflect questions that I'm uncomfortable answering."

He leaned a shoulder against the doorjamb.

"Remind me to warn Ty not to try and put anything over on you when he lands in your class eight or nine years from now."

"That's the thing. Adults are just big kids. Human nature doesn't change even when maturity sets in. And your nature is all about turning your back on emotions."

"Okay. Now I forgot the question."

"No, you didn't. But I'll remind you anyway because now I'm even more curious. Do you like Kate?"

"Define 'like.'"

Her eyes narrowed. "Don't make me send you to the principal's office."

"Okay." He held up his hands in surrender. "Let's just say I've noticed that she's not hard on the eyes."

"I'll take that as a yes." She nodded, looking pleased. "It hasn't happened to you since your wife left, and that scares the crap out of you."

"Watch it, Caroline. I'm a guy. Nothing scares me."

"No," she agreed. "Unless you're talking about personal feelings and commitment. And who could blame you? The only thing more scary to a guy than talking about feelings is being solely responsible for an infant, the way you were when your wife left. I've got news for you, Cabot. If a woman has no experience with a baby, she's just as scared as you were with that little boy."

"What about the maternal instinct?" He'd often wondered what Ty was missing out on without having his mom.

"I'm not sure. I just know being scared isn't gender specific when it comes to babies."

"You?" He didn't believe she was afraid of anything.

"Oh, yeah. When Jake was born, I'd never held a newborn before, let alone been primarily responsible for keeping one alive." She shook her head ruefully at the memory. "And I had a husband to help. God bless Nolan. The night we brought our son home, the baby was crying. I was crying. Nolan told me to go to bed and he'd make sure the little guy was okay. And he did."

"Good man."

"No argument here. But you didn't have anyone when Jennifer walked out. And you had a ranch to run, not a nine-to-five job. No one can blame you for not ever wanting to be that vulnerable again."

"So, you're not going to tell me to get over

it and take a chance? Get back up on the horse?"

"I'd be lying if I said I don't want to. Part of me does." She sighed. "But mostly I don't want to see you hurt like that ever again."

Cabot would second that motion. "Then why are we having this conversation about whether I like Kate?"

"Because I've seen the way you look at her. Ty, too. The Dixon men both have a crush on that runaway bride. That alone should make you take off in the other direction."

"So, you don't like her."

"I didn't say that." Caroline folded her arms over her chest. "I actually like her quite a bit. She's a hard worker. Funny. Very pretty. But—"

"What?"

"She's got secrets. And not about that jerk she left at the altar."

"And you know this—how?"

"When you've worked with teenagers as long as I have, you learn to spot that in a person. Not saying the secret is a bad thing. Or a good thing, for that matter. Just that she's hiding something. I wanted to give you my take on that."

"Okay. Consider it shared." He started to

turn away, then remembered why he was here. "How are the kids? Rain can put a damper, no pun, on outdoor activities."

"Jim and his staff have it covered. They're showing videos, playing board games and doing crafts. Indoor stuff. The usual."

"At least they have an extra pair of hands with Kate here to fill in when someone needs a break."

"True—" She stopped. "Except, now that I think about it, she should be back by now."

"Where is she?"

"I sent her into Blackwater Lake with a short list of a few things I needed for the breakfast menu. But that was a couple of hours ago."

"Maybe she came back and is with the other counselors and the kids," he suggested.

Caroline shook her head. "She'd have dropped the groceries off here first. No. I hope nothing's wrong."

"Don't borrow trouble."

"Can't help it. I'm wired that way." She shrugged. "Just have a feeling."

"I'll go look for her."

"Thanks, Cabot. That would make me feel better."

"Don't mention it."

He left Caroline at her desk and trudged back up to the house, where his truck was parked. He got in out of the rain and, after fishing the keys out of his pocket, turned on the ignition. The engine roared to life and he backed out of the space, then headed slowly up the road. Worry nagged at him—partly for Kate's safety, but partly something else.

The first thing he'd learned about her was that she'd run away. Caroline had just reminded him about that. It crossed his mind that she might have run out now, and the thought tied him in knots. That realization proved his control over this attraction thing wasn't nearly as tight as he'd wanted to believe.

Only one road could take him into town, so if she was stuck or out of gas, he couldn't miss her. Proving his point, a couple of miles from the ranch he spotted a lone figure walking toward him. A closer look told him it was Kate and she was soaked.

He stopped the truck beside her and hit the button to roll down his window. "Hop in."

She nodded and walked around the front of the vehicle. It was bad enough that she was shivering, which made him want to strip off her clothes and hold her close to warm her. But she was wearing a white T-shirt that might as well be invisible because it was wet and nearly transparent. Thank God she was wearing a bra, although he could make out the size and shape of her breasts.

He put the truck in Park and released his seat belt, then slipped off his slicker. When she was in the passenger seat, he said, "Put this on. It will help a little. I'll have you back to your cabin in ten minutes."

"O—okay." She slid her arms into the too-big coat and pulled it closed.

Everything that made his mouth water was covered, but some sights you couldn't un-see or convince yourself that you didn't want to see more.

"What happened?" There was nothing the least bit gentle in his tone and he was really sorry about that.

"T—truck broke down halfway to town—" An attack of shivers stopped her. "No idea what's wrong with it. But do you realize there's not a lot of traffic on this road?"

"Yeah."

"I forgot my cell phone. So I finally decided to walk."

"Now you're soaked to the skin." He

burned all over just from saying the word. "You should have stayed in the truck."

"I did that, but clearly there's no traffic on this road. I finally decided to walk back for help because I thought Caroline might need the things on the list."

"She can work around them," he snapped. "No one's going to starve."

"I don't know why you're so crabby."

Worry did that to a man. And she wasn't the first female that day to wonder about his mood. "Let's just call it PMS."

"Oo-kay."

At least that shut her up for the rest of the drive. When they got back to the ranch, he drove her straight to her cabin. "Get dry clothes on."

"Really? You think I require an order for that?" She shot him a look. "Because I look like I enjoy being soaked?"

No. Because he couldn't handle much more of knowing that underneath the slicker he'd given her there was a wet T-shirt that clung to her breasts.

"You'll be more comfortable when I take you into town to get that stuff for Caroline and arrange to have your truck fixed."

"Give me five minutes," she said and hopped out.

He blew out a long breath and rubbed the back of his neck. The quicker she put on dry clothes, the sooner he would stop thinking about getting her naked. Possibly he would even stop aching to touch her bare silky skin.

Maybe, but not likely.

Chapter Eight

Cabot's crabby mood didn't improve on the way to Blackwater Lake. Kate had made several attempts at chitchat, but his one-word answers didn't invite conversation. It probably didn't help that she'd kept him waiting longer than five minutes. The lure of a hot shower had been a temptation she couldn't ignore. It was one thing to get soaking wet in the rain and quite another to do it under a hot spray. She'd been freezing, and that was the quickest way to warm up. Now her hair was pulled into a ponytail and she was wearing dry jeans with a camp T-shirt. No makeup. Because Cabot was driving her to town, she'd been tempted to put on mascara and lipstick, but there hadn't been time. He didn't look like a man who wanted to be kept waiting.

On the road they passed the sad truck. She had no idea why her brother had such an attachment to the thing, including naming it Angelica, but he was a man. Who knew why they made certain choices?

Case in point… She glanced over at Cabot. Why didn't he let one of the ranch hands drive her into town to pick up things for Caroline and take care of her dead truck? Clearly Cabot didn't want to be here, so why had he chosen to come?

Darned if Kate knew. She just wanted to take care of business and get back to the kids. They were much less complicated and a lot more fun.

"We're going to stop at McKnight's Auto Repair."

For groceries, she wanted to say. But he wasn't in the mood for jokes. She was in the mood to poke the bear just a little, though. "Aren't you going to tell me it's the best place in town?"

"It's the *only* place in town." He glanced over. "But Tom McKnight is honest and good at what he does. He taught his daughter, Sydney, everything she knows. Between the two of them, I don't think there's anything they can't fix."

"Is Sydney McKnight the son her parents never had?"

"Well, her mother died when she was born. And since she has two older brothers, I'd have to say no to the son thing."

Wow, she'd never known her mom. Kate couldn't imagine growing up without her own mother. The woman had been her anchor every time the family moved when the army reassigned her dad.

"Maybe she's competing with her brothers for her father's attention."

"Don't tell me. You were a shrink in your other life."

"No." At least she'd gotten him talking. "I'm just wondering why a woman would choose a career working on cars."

"Family business."

Hmm. Apparently he wasn't the only one pressured into taking over. "Why didn't her brothers go to work in the garage?"

"Ben McKnight is an orthopedist who works at Mercy Medical Clinic. His brother, Alex, owns a construction company."

"So Sydney was forced into it." She looked at Cabot and saw a muscle in his jaw jerk.

"I can't picture Tom McKnight laying a guilt trip on any of his kids. He's salt of the earth and just wanted them to do whatever would make them happy." He met her gaze for a moment. "I also can't see Syd doing something she doesn't want to."

"You must know her pretty well."

"Yeah."

And they were back to one-word answers. In the silence, Kate's thoughts turned to the female mechanic and how *well* Cabot knew her. If Kate had to put a finer point on the feeling squeezing her chest, she would call it jealousy. That was stupid, so she decided not to define what she was feeling.

But she couldn't stop wondering. Caroline had said he discreetly dated, and Sydney was certainly handy. But, seriously, a female mechanic? Grease, dirt, engines? What kind of woman would want to…?

That was where she stopped herself. People could say the same thing about her and why she would want to take part in skeet-shooting competitions. The saying about glass houses and throwing stones came to mind.

And then they were driving down Main

Street in the town of Blackwater Lake. Every time she saw it, the charm of the place pulled her in a little deeper. They passed the Grizzly Bear Diner. Beside it was Potter's Ice Cream Parlor and Tanya's Treasures, a souvenir and gift store. The Grocery Store came up on the left and again she felt as if the combination of businesses and residential areas made up a magical village surrounded by evergreen trees to protect it from encroaching civilization.

"There's McKnight's," Cabot said. "Just up ahead on the left."

As they got closer, Kate decided it looked pretty much like any other garage she'd ever seen—an office connected by an overhang to the work area, where vehicles were elevated on hydraulic lifts so the mechanic could easily look underneath. A tow truck took up a parking space and sported the business name and phone number on the side door. The building was white with royal-blue trim, and a sign visible from the street declared in bold black letters McKnight's Auto Repair.

The rain hadn't stopped, so Cabot pulled up and stopped beneath the overhang outside the office. "I'll introduce you."

"Okay."

As she slid out of his truck, a man somewhere in his late fifties walked out of the office. He was tall, handsome and distinguished looking with a full head of silver hair.

Cabot walked over to him, hand extended. “Hi, Tom. How are you?”

“Great. Good to see you, Cabot.” His gaze settled on her.

“This is Kate Scott.”

She smiled. “Nice to meet you, Mr. McKnight.”

“Call me Tom.” He was friendly and easygoing, and then something that looked a lot like recognition slid into his eyes. “Aren’t you the runaway bride I heard about?”

Kate was relieved that he’d referenced her first day in town and not recognition for her accomplishments in the sporting world and her outdoor endorsements. “That depends on what you heard. If it was good, then I’m the one.”

The older man laughed. “Nice to meet you.”

“Kate had a problem with her truck,” Cabot explained. “It died on the road from the ranch into town.”

“Sorry to hear that,” Tom said. “We’ll get it towed in and have a look. See what we can do.”

"I'd appreciate that. It's pretty old but has a lot of sentimental value." At least that was her guess. Why else would her brother hang on to it? He could easily afford a new truck to have around for the convenience of transporting stuff that wouldn't fit into his expensive sports car.

"If anyone can get it going, Syd can. That's my daughter," the older man explained.

The door behind him had opened and a young woman came out just in time to hear what he'd said. She had a bottle of water in her hand. "What can I do?"

This stunning woman was Sydney McKnight, girl mechanic? Kate had stereotyped her until this very second. She'd expected a bigger woman, someone less delicate. For several moments, she stared and sincerely hoped that her mouth hadn't dropped open.

"I was just saying you can fix pretty much any car—old, new and in-between."

"Thanks, Dad." She took a sip from her water. "Hey, Cabot. Haven't seen you for ages. How's Ty?"

"Great. No offense, Syd, but I'm glad I haven't seen you on a professional call."

Kate literally felt the tension drain from her body. If they hadn't seen each other for ages, that meant this beautiful woman wasn't dating him. They acted more like brother and sister. Either that or the two of them were very good liars, but she didn't believe that was the case.

"Who's this?" Sydney asked, looking at her.

Kate had a feeling she already knew. Still, she stuck out her hand. "Kate Scott, the infamous runaway bride."

"Nice to meet you." The other woman grinned and squeezed her fingers.

She was wearing a light blue shirt with the business logo and her name embroidered on it tucked into the waistband of navy work pants. Steel-toed boots completed the ensemble. Sydney made it look almost chic. She was petite and curvy with dark hair pulled into a ponytail. Wisps and curls had escaped to charmingly frame her delicate face and make her big brown eyes look even bigger. They were snapping with intelligence and curiosity.

"Nice to see you, Syd." Cabot started toward the office. "If it's all right with you, Tom, I'd like to get the paperwork going on Kate's truck."

"We'll get it taken care of," the older man said to her.

"Thanks." She started to follow him into the office.

"Got this covered," Cabot told her.

"But it's my responsibility to take care of it."

"Stay here and talk to Syd."

"I'd like that. After I make arrangements for the truck. Cabot?"

The men had disappeared inside. Her words had not slowed them down.

"You just got the equivalent of don't-worry-your-pretty-little-head." Sydney was amused.

"I noticed. You know, sometimes it's annoying," Kate observed. "But with cars and bugs and a few other things, not so much. Men can be handy to have around."

"I know what you mean." Sydney sized her up. "So, was it those other things or the annoying part that made you run out on the wedding?"

"I guess there's no point in expecting that the runaway-bride label will ever be forgotten here in Blackwater Lake?"

"Not likely. I'm pretty sure the story will take on legend status in the annals of Blackwater Lake folklore." Sydney's gaze was penetrating. "Why did you run?"

"He was a cheating weasel. I walked in

on him kissing one of my bridesmaids at the church on the day of."

Anger mixed with understanding in the other woman's eyes and turned them a darker shade of brown. "Why do the backstabbing bastards steal from our pool of friends? Why can't they just go swimming with a perfect stranger?"

"Is that a rhetorical question?"

Syd looked thoughtful for a moment, then nodded solemnly. "Yes."

"It happened to you, too, didn't it?"

The other woman shrugged. "Even Blackwater Lake has its share of jerks."

An understanding expression in Sydney McKnight's eyes convinced Kate she'd been through a similar experience.

"Whoever he is, I hope he rots in hell," Kate said vehemently.

"If only." Her mouth pulled tight for a moment before letting go of the bad memory. "Have you met many people in town yet?"

"No. I've been busy." *And reverting to the learned childhood behavior of not getting close to anyone because I won't be staying.*

Sydney tapped her lip, studying her. "You look really familiar. Have you ever been to Blackwater Lake before?"

Kate shook her head. It could be that the other woman had seen her in a magazine or TV ad. She was, after all, the face of a well-known outdoor-equipment company. But if the cat wasn't out of the bag yet, she would like to keep it there for a little while longer. Not being recognized was a lovely change.

"I guess I just have one of those faces. Or, as they say, everyone has a twin." Kate shrugged.

"Maybe," Sydney said without much conviction. "The thing is, I'd like to get to know you better. We should have a girls' night out."

"Sounds good." And she meant that. It wasn't often you met someone and clicked, but she felt that with this woman. "The counselors at the summer camp rotate an evening off during the week."

"Dad and I do that, too. And since he started dating someone, I can't just ask him to cover for me."

"You think he'd mind, just one night?"

"No. He just doesn't know I know that he's got a woman. First one since my mom died."

Because she'd brought it up, Kate felt she could ask. "Cabot said you never knew your mother."

"That's right. She died giving birth to me."

The emotion in her voice was no more than if she'd just said the sun was hot.

"It's all right, Kate. I never knew her. It's hard to mourn someone you didn't have a relationship with. Plus, it was a long time ago."

"Sorry." Kate hadn't been aware that her thoughts showed so clearly on her face. Then it sank in that Syd was in her mid to late twenties and the picture came together. "You mean your dad hasn't gone out with a woman in all these years?"

"If he did, no one knew. And he's not covert-operations material, although he really believes he's covered his tracks this time and no one is the wiser." She grinned a little wickedly. "I'm curious about how long he can keep up the charade. When it's out, I can tell him how much I just want him to be happy."

"That's hilarious and sweet in equal parts." Kate grinned at her. "Men think they're so cool about this stuff."

"Or hot." Sydney's eyes narrowed. "So we're clear, now I'm talking about the way that handsome rancher looks at you."

"Cabot?" She could see him through the window at the service desk inside. "Either you're imagining that or it's because he's irritated with me."

"Anger and affection are flip sides of the same coin and touch somewhere in the middle."

"Did you get that out of a fortune cookie?" Kate teased.

"No. I think I heard it somewhere." Sydney grinned. "But, seriously, the sort of looks he was giving you could burn up the sheets."

Kate made light of the comments, but that didn't stop her from wondering. Since he'd apologized for kissing her, his vow not to do it again had been in jeopardy only that one time in the barn, when Ty had schemed to get the two of them alone. But that didn't stop her from hoping.

She really wanted another opportunity to see if she was simply inventing the passion she'd felt in his kiss or if there was a real possibility of getting swept away.

"I really like Sydney McKnight." Kate hauled herself into the passenger seat of Cabot's truck, then slammed the door shut.

"She's good people." He put the key in the ignition and, unlike her vehicle, it roared to life.

The two of them had made arrangements for McKnight's Auto Repair to tow her truck from the side of the road to their shop. After they looked it over to diagnose the problem, she'd get a call about the estimate for repairs. Hopefully Angelica was fixable and parts for the old girl were available. Then she thought about how Cabot had described Sydney.

She's good people.

Kate had been curious about the female mechanic before meeting her and was even more interested now. How had he meant that? Sydney was a very pretty young woman, and if a guy liked cars, she would be a hot ticket. She would be even if a guy didn't like cars. Although Kate figured her boss as more of a horse guy, her female radar was shooting out signals like crazy. Signals that felt suspiciously like jealousy even though the two of them seemed nothing more than friends.

"How well do you know her?" Kate asked.

"I don't know." He checked traffic on Main Street, then pulled out of the lot and stopped at the signal. "She was born and raised here. So was I."

That was the opposite of helpful when what she wanted was details. Was there ever anything romantic between them? Like had they ever gone out? But she couldn't ask that.

And yet the words came out of her mouth. “So, did you two ever go out?”

The light changed and he accelerated. “No.”

“Why not?” She wasn’t going to let him out of answering that easily.

“I was friends with her brothers.”

“Which would make her like a little sister.”

“Yes.”

He was going to have to stop being so stingy with details so she could find out what she wanted to know more quickly and efficiently. “Do you think she’s pretty?”

“I’ve never given it much thought.” He turned right into the grocery-store parking lot and found a space.

After sliding out of the truck, Kate fell into step beside him. “So, think about it now.”

“Why?” He scowled at her. “You’re like a dog with a favorite bone.”

“I’m curious about your type.”

“Given my lousy track record with women,” he said grimly, “if I had a type and decided to be involved with someone, I’d look for the exact opposite.”

“So you would ignore a woman you’re attracted to and gravitate toward one you don’t like?”

"Always a good rule."

Hmm. He was systematically and thoroughly ignoring *her,* so apparently that was a compliment.

He grabbed a grocery cart and rolled it past the glass doors that automatically opened for them. "You got that list Caroline gave you?"

"Yes. It's a little damp, but I think I can still read what she wrote."

They moved quickly through the store, grabbing pancake mix, syrup, cereal and a few other things. Fortunately the place stocked the large industrial sizes, but that was probably because ranches were in the area and the owners liked to buy in bulk. To stock up for emergencies, she'd been told, like getting snowed in.

At checkout the clerk scanned everything and gave Cabot a total, which he put on a credit card. When the items were bagged and in the cart, he wheeled it out to the truck, then put the bags in the rear seat while she got in the front. He stowed the cart so it wouldn't roll into another car, then slid into the driver's seat. After starting the engine, he looked over his shoulder to check for other vehicles. When the coast was clear, he backed out and headed for the exit.

"So, about Sydney—"

"You better be talking about Australia." His face wasn't visible because he was looking away to make sure there was a break in traffic, but his voice was full of irritation. "What's with you, anyway?"

"I'm curious. Sue me." She was enjoying this more than she should be. "She's an above-average-looking woman and you're not hard on the eyes. Just saying…"

"Just *stop* saying." He glared at her. "Syd is way too smart to hook up with me. Besides, she's had her own romantic disaster—"

"What happened to her?"

"No, you don't. I'm not getting sucked into gossip. Not spreading it."

"But where's the harm? I'm leaving at the end of summer."

"Doesn't matter. In the spirit of discretion and setting a good example, my answer is that if you want to know what happened to Sydney, you'll have to ask her."

"All right," she said. "I'll do that. We're going to get together soon. So there."

"Okay, then."

Kate was surprised when after driving a short way down Main he pulled into a parking space in front of Blackwater Lake Sporting

Goods Warehouse. "Why are you stopping here?"

"I need a couple things. Might as well get them while we're in town." He looked at her. "You in a hurry to get back?"

"Caroline might need me."

"She'll call if she does." He ended the conversation by getting out of the truck.

"Okay, then." She followed him inside.

A friendly-looking middle-aged man stood at the cash register just inside the door. He glanced up from something he was reading when they walked in and smiled. "Hey, Cabot. Haven't seen you in a while."

"Nolan." He shook the other man's hand. "Been pretty busy."

"How's Ty?"

"Great. Getting big." He must have sensed her waiting for an introduction. "Nolan Daly, this is Kate Scott."

"You look familiar," he said, trying to place her.

"I guess I just have one of those faces." She shrugged, then changed the subject. "You're Caroline's husband. I really like working with her at the camp. It's very nice to meet you."

"Caro told me about you. How do you like it here in Blackwater Lake?" Like his wife, he used reading glasses and perched them on the end of his nose.

He didn't say anything about her being a runaway bride. Maybe it was possible to live that down. "It's a really nice place. I love the lake and mountains. I can truthfully say that I've never seen anywhere prettier."

"You traveled much?"

"Actually—" she met Cabot's gaze "—I have. All over the world. I'm an army brat, after all."

"You like what you're doing at the summer camp?"

She knew the store owner was really asking what she did for a living before running out on her wedding. Fortunately the phone rang and she didn't have to give him an answer.

Cabot looked at her. "I'll go grab what I need."

"Do you mind if I look around?"

"Suit yourself. Meet you back here in fifteen minutes."

She nodded and they parted ways. Kate headed to the women's outdoor-clothing section. She browsed through fleece jackets and knit shirts displayed on racks. One of the brands was a company she'd done some modeling for, lending the name of an Olympic medalist to their product.

"Cute," she said to herself, holding up a pink, long-sleeved V-neck shirt.

Next she looked through a rack of knit hats. If she were staying in Blackwater Lake for winter, she would need one, but not for California, unless she went skiing in the mountains.

They had a good selection of running and hiking shoes and boots. Warm socks were on display nearby. She didn't realize how much time had passed until she glanced at her watch.

"Uh-oh." She hurried back to the front, where Cabot was flipping through one of the outdoor magazines displayed in a wire rack by the cash register. All she could see was his profile, but as she moved closer, it looked as if his jaw was clenched.

He must have heard her approach and looked up. "See anything?"

"Why?" She thought there was something weird in his tone.

"I sure did." He held up the magazine. On the cover was a picture of her in a bikini, holding a fishing rod. "You're not who I thought you were."

Chapter Nine

Cabot watched Kate's eyes narrow and knew some sassy words were coming his way. Oddly, he was looking forward to it.

"I told you I wasn't who you thought, but you insisted on believing what you wanted. I never lied to you about needing a break to get my life together."

"You also never gave me any details about the life you needed a break from."

Looking away for a moment, she pressed her lips together. "I had my reasons."

"It's about time you share them." He could almost feel Nolan behind them watching this unfold, listening to every word.

"Okay. The short version is that I've won several Olympic medals for skeet shooting. That led to product-endorsement contracts. In certain outdoor-enthusiast circles, I'm somewhat well-known."

"I knew you looked familiar." Both of them turned toward Nolan Daly, who was looking a little starstruck.

"You know her?" Cabot asked.

"Yes. Katrina Scott. Can't believe I didn't put the name and face together when we were introduced. Except the Kate part threw me off and maybe that picture of you on the magazine cover was a distraction."

Cabot knew what he meant. The photo of her in a bikini revealed curves that he'd only felt through her clothes. That was temptation enough, but putting that memory with the visual might be his undoing. "How do you know her?"

The man set his reading glasses beside the bagged merchandise on the counter. "I follow the major shooting competitions, and this young lady has quite the reputation. Second-youngest woman ever to medal when she was just a teenager. And she did it again at two more games."

Cabot met her gaze. "Impressive."

"Thank you."

Nolan reached over the counter and picked up one of the magazines from the display. "Miss Scott, would you mind signing this for me?"

"It's Kate, and I'd be happy to, Mr. Daly."

"Nolan, please. It's a real honor to meet you."

She smiled. "The pleasure is mine."

"Wait until I tell Caroline about this," he said. "She has no idea who you are. An Olympic medalist here in Blackwater Lake, right under our noses."

"I've really enjoyed the peace and quiet here."

Cabot heard the regret in her voice and noted her use of past tense. The peace and quiet would be over now that she'd been outed. She was an Olympic medalist, not an Academy Award–winning actress who could manufacture emotions. She was telling the truth. It wasn't his proudest moment when the realization hit that he'd wanted her to be a stray, someone who needed his help. Someone he'd never compromise with messy complications.

Now he couldn't hide behind that to resist her. He was his father's son; wanting Kate was proof that he did possess the Dixon

DNA that predisposed him to be attracted to women who would leave.

"Well..." Cabot put the magazine away, then picked up his purchases off the counter. "We better be going."

"Nice to meet you, Kate."

Her smile looked a lot like the cover-girl one—it didn't reach her eyes. "Nice to meet you, too."

"Come in again."

Cabot put the bags in the backseat of the truck while Kate climbed inside. When everything was stowed, he got in beside her.

"Want to get a bite to eat before we go back?"

"Why?" It was a tie as to whether her tone or expression was more wary.

"Because you're hungry?"

"I can eat with the kids. And we have to get the groceries back to Caroline."

"There's nothing she needs tonight, and all of it is nonperishable." He turned the key in the ignition. "I'd like to talk to you."

Technically he didn't have to buy her a meal to do that. They'd had a number of conversations, one that had ended with a kiss, and there hadn't been food involved at all.

"What about Ty?" she asked.

He glanced at his watch. "He's getting

picked up right about now for a sleepover at C.J.'s. So, what do you say?"

"You're the boss." At least for now. She didn't say that out loud, but her tone clearly implied it.

He debated the pros and cons of going to the Grizzly Bear Diner. The two of them together would trigger talk, but that was going to happen anyway, what with this trip to town.

"What's wrong, Kate?"

"So many things, so little time." She glanced over at him. "Mostly it's about the fact that word about me will spread and everything will change. It was nice when I knew that someone liked me for me and not because I have a certain celebrity."

Cabot couldn't say that his feelings hadn't changed at all. He'd been attracted the first moment they'd met and still was. If only the truth had neutralized his interest in her.

After parking in the lot behind the diner, they went inside and were seated right away at a booth in the back. The place, decorated with pictures of bears on the walls, wasn't crowded yet. It was late for the lunch crowd and early for dinner. A waitress handed them menus, then said she'd give them a few minutes.

Kate's expression was guarded. "There's no reason for you to get angry and defensive."

He pushed the menu aside because he always ordered the same thing. "Who says I am?"

"Like I said before, I never lied to you."

"If anyone is defensive, it's you," he pointed out.

"I'm trying not to get fired."

"Clearly you really don't need the money, so why do you care?" He studied her, the bruised look and big eyes. "The cat is out of the bag. The word will be all over Blackwater Lake in a day. Two, tops. What difference does it make if folks know your story?"

"The difference is that the campers have no idea who I am and don't care. I forgot what it felt like to be judged on my work and not like someone who's been in the news." She met his gaze. "Don't get me wrong. I'm not complaining. I've been lucky and I'm not one of those people who gripe that the crown is too tight, the jewels too heavy. It took practice, dedication and sacrifice to achieve what I have. Also a lot of hard work. And luck. I'm grateful for everything. It's just that circumstances presented themselves and along came a chance to be anonymous."

"Circumstances? Meaning running out on a wedding?" He deliberately brought that up, trying to rekindle resentment and remind himself she was a runner. That should be enough to make him avoid her, but apparently he needed more.

"Yeah, the wedding that didn't happen." She opened the menu but didn't look at it. "He's a sports agent and contacted me after my repeat medal performance. I was a media darling and he convinced me to sign while I was hot."

Past tense? To Cabot's way of thinking, she was still hot, but that wasn't what she meant. "And?"

"He got me lucrative endorsement deals and magazine shoots. In the outdoor-equipment business I'm a spokesperson, and I'm well paid for it. He got a piece of that, but apparently it wasn't enough. The marriage would have given him financial security that his percentage didn't. But, also apparent to everyone but me, he was unwilling to give up the other women."

"I see." Creep, he thought. Her expression tugged at him. Was it anger, hurt or both?

"Cabot, there was bound to be media hype after I walked out on the wedding. I'd just seen him kissing someone I considered a friend. I was emotionally raw and just plain tired. Instinct made me run, but eventually it turned into an opportunity for the story to cool off and for me to get out of the fast lane for a while." Sincerity was all over her face. "Now I just want to finish what I started. Make it to the end of the summer with the kids. I love working with them."

"Okay." He believed her. "For the record, I never planned to fire you."

"Then why did you bring me here?" she asked, looking around the diner.

"So I can say that I'm the guy who bought you your first Grizzly Bear burger." He shrugged. "Claim to fame."

She laughed and nodded. "Okay, then."

It wasn't okay, but it was the best he could do. She was right. He didn't have to bring her here. After that kiss he'd been doing his best to avoid her and was at a loss as to why he'd invited her to dinner.

If he was being honest with himself, part of the reason was that he wanted to postpone taking her back to her cabin, then going into his empty house alone. The other part was a risk, pure and simple.

He couldn't shake his inconvenient and unwelcome attraction to her, and the avoidance strategy wasn't working. Maybe it would be better to confront the situation, go with it and get her out of his system once and for all.

After two glasses of wine at the Grizzly Bear Diner, Kate was rocking a little buzz as she rode back to the ranch in the passenger seat of Cabot's truck. She'd had a really nice time with him, which she hadn't expected. She'd figured he'd be tense and disapproving after finding out she wasn't a stray he needed to take under his wing, at least not financially. Emotionally was a different story.

He'd taken her in and given her refuge, a quiet place to nurse the bruises of public humiliation. She would always be grateful to him for that.

Word would spread in Blackwater Lake about who she was, and she didn't mind too much, proving that she was strong enough now to deal with the mess she'd left behind. When the summer was over, she would take care of that. For now, she was enjoying the heck out of being here and working with the kids. She wasn't looking forward to this pause coming to an end.

"So," she said, glancing over at him. "I had

a much better time at the diner today than the day I first walked in."

"That was an interesting moment for Blackwater Lake." Just enough moon shone in the truck windows for her to make out his grin.

Desire hit her—sudden and irresistible. Without the chip on his shoulder, he'd been funny and charming, different from the guarded man she was accustomed to seeing. And she'd been attracted to that man with the chronic brooding expression, maybe because of it. But this guy who smiled and laughed, the one who spread around charm like butter on toast, really cranked up the fascination factor.

"It must be nice to go out and know everyone and they know you."

"It has pros and cons."

"Like what?" she asked.

"You don't always appreciate folks knowing your business, but if you ever need a hand, it's usually not necessary to ask for it."

"I like that." Cozy and calm, she leaned her head against the high seat back. "Bad stuff happens, but it's probably a comfort to not feel alone when it does."

"Did you run because you felt alone?" She heard a rasp in his voice, just a hint that he might be a little irritated about what had happened to her.

"I didn't mean to sound pathetic. And my family is supportive, but sometimes protecting them means going it alone. Without anyone to share the burden."

"What did you think of the Mama Bear Burger?"

His question lightened the mood, as if he knew she was going to a pensive place and made a deliberate effort to pull her back from the edge. That was so nice. And sensitive.

"Please don't tell Caroline because she does amazing things with a ground-beef patty—"

"I hear a 'but.'"

She laughed. "*But* I've been to some gourmet hamburger places in L.A. and Las Vegas that were good. But that Mama Bear has to be one of the best I've ever had."

"I know you told Michelle that, but you can be honest with me. We're alone now."

Yes, they were, and it was best not to dwell on that too much.

Michelle had stopped by their booth tonight. She'd said it was customer service, to make sure everything was okay, but Kate was pretty sure the move had been motivated by curiosity. The woman hadn't laid eyes on her since the day Kate had walked in wearing a wedding gown and Cabot had hired her on the spot. Now they'd come in together for dinner. Who wouldn't want more information?

"This is the honest truth—it was a straight-up juicy, thick patty without sauces and distractions that mask the flavor. I loved it. And those big, fat fries are my favorite. Trust me on this—I know my potatoes. I'm a connoisseur."

"Ty likes the fries, too. And the Bear Cub chicken fingers."

"It's a very cute place. Great atmosphere. And quite a nice wine selection."

"It will be a while before he'll be able to have an opinion on that."

There was that devastating smile for the second time, and again she felt the difference in him. He was more relaxed, not pushing back against the natural give-and-take between them. Maybe she should have given him details about herself sooner. But he probably wouldn't have believed her.

Maybe he didn't care enough to look her name up on Google. Or maybe he cared too much.

Tingles danced through her, and she was pretty sure it had nothing to do with the wine.

The sooner she got out of this truck, the better. He'd made it clear that there was a line between boss and employee that shouldn't be crossed. She didn't want to slip up and jeopardize this budding friendship.

"He's a great kid," she said. "You've done a wonderful job with him."

"I appreciate you saying so. It hasn't been easy—no two ways about that. But he is, without a doubt, the best thing that ever happened to me."

Kate wondered yet again how a woman could turn her back on her own baby. And walk away from a good man like Cabot Dixon. He was honest, hardworking and capable of deep feeling—not like anyone she'd ever met, and she figured it was doubtful she would run across his like again.

Just in the nick of time, before any of that could come out of her mouth, Cabot drove underneath the sign that said Dixon Ranch and Summer Camp.

The headlights picked out puddles still scattered over the dirt road from the earlier rainstorm. He pulled to a stop by the big house and turned off the engine. A lot had happened since her soaking earlier that day, and things felt different, a sign that she needed to get back to her cabin ASAP.

"Thanks for taking me into town and helping deal with my truck."

"Anytime."

"I'll grab those groceries and drop them by the kitchen on the way to my cabin."

But before she could open the truck's rear passenger door, Cabot was beside her. "Leave them."

"But Caroline needs the stuff for breakfast."

"I'll make sure she gets it." He moved close and his breath stirred wisps of hair around her face.

"Cabot, we shouldn't— You said—"

He touched a finger to her mouth, instantly stopping the flow of words. "I was wrong."

The softness of his voice did nothing to diminish the intensity of his tone. And then he kissed her.

Kate sighed and, in spite of her protest, relaxed against him. With his arms around her to cushion her, he backed her against the truck, making the contact of their bodies closer. They were a surprisingly good fit; it would only be better if they were horizontal.

He proceeded to kiss the breath out of her

and didn't stop the resistance-shattering assault even as she moaned against his mouth. He traced her lips with his tongue, and she opened to him without hesitation. Boldly, he dipped inside and showed her what he would do if he made love to her.

Finally he came up for air, the sound of his heavy breathing harsh in the clear night air. "Kate, I want to take you upstairs to my bed—"

And she wanted badly to say yes, but...

Cupping her hand to his cheek, she felt the scrape of stubble on his jaw. Absurdly she thought how fast his beard had grown in the hours since he'd shaved that morning. It was sexy and stoked the heat of desire building inside her.

"Cabot," she finally managed to say, "this isn't smart."

"Probably not. But then, no one has ever accused me of being too smart." As he turned his mouth into her palm, the words caressed the sensitive skin.

She sucked in a breath. "I'm trying to be strong."

"It's not that I don't appreciate what you're saying, but right this minute I'd rather not talk."

"Are you sure you want to start something?"

"I'll tell you what I'm sure about. We're just a man and woman who want each other. Nothing more."

"Nothing less," she whispered. "Safe."

"Yes." He regarded her with impatience and heat swirling in his eyes, but he said nothing else to sway her one way or the other. No pressure.

And there didn't need to be. She wanted him, too. "I wish I could say you're wrong."

His smile was full of satisfaction and he simply held out his hand. She put her fingers into his palm and let him lead her up the front steps and into the house.

Cabot turned on a light just inside the entryway, revealing the need in his eyes. Without letting go of her hand, he guided her up the stairs to the second door on the left—his bedroom. He flipped the wall switch and the room lit up.

A four-poster pine bed was straight ahead with a matching dresser and armoire on adjacent walls. A doorway to the left was probably the bathroom, and French doors opened to a balcony that from this orientation would have a spectacular view of the lake and towering mountains. It was a big room and definitely a *man's* space.

"This suits you," she said.

"*You* suit me." His voice was hoarse with desire.

A woman wasn't living here now, but his wife must have once upon a time. And no doubt after her abandonment he'd brought women here, on those nights his son was having a sleepover at a friend's house. But Kate couldn't deal with any of that. Didn't want to. For so long she'd done everything by the book, followed the rules, thought all decisions to death. Her life had been structured every minute of every day.

All she wanted now was something spontaneous and just for her. She had to believe that sometimes it was all right to be selfish.

"Earth to Kate…" Cabot leaned over and gently kissed her with no other parts of their bodies touching.

It was so sweet and provocative at the same time that she ached to be as close as a man and woman could get. She stood on tiptoe and wrapped her arms around his neck, and the movement was like tossing a match on dry leaves. She was ready to ignite, and tension in his body was a clear indication that he felt the same.

Cabot tugged at her shirt as she undid the snaps on his. She toed off her sneakers, and he yanked his boots, then tossed them aside. The harsh sound of their mingled breathing filled the room as the rest of their clothes joined the growing pile.

He tugged her to the side of the bed and tossed back the comforter, blanket and sheet in a single, powerful move. Then he grabbed her to him and turned his body so that she fell on top of him when they tumbled together onto the mattress. The power position lasted all of a nanosecond as he rolled her onto her back and nestled beside her.

The feel of his bare skin was intoxicating and the dusting of hair on his chest teased her breasts. He kissed her mouth, cheek, jaw and neck as his hand slid past the curve of her waist, over her hip and down her leg.

Then he turned his attention to the inside of her thigh. The featherlight touch sent a shaft of heat straight to her feminine core and he never stopped kissing her. Men were notorious for not multitasking well, but he seemed to be doing all right. His fingers inched higher, and anticipation flowed through her, waiting for him to touch the most sensitive of places. When he did, she nearly whimpered from the exquisite torture of it all.

"You're so soft," he whispered against her neck. "And you smell good, like flowers."

He smelled good, too, and the strength in his arms and chest were undeniable, but he held her as if she were a delicate, pricey piece of porcelain. That was such a turn-on.

"Cabot—" She arched her hips against his hand, letting him know without words what she craved.

She was nearly to the point of begging when he shifted slightly and reached into the nightstand drawer to pull out a small, square packet. Later she would be grateful he'd remembered protection, but right this second, all she could say was "Hurry."

"Doing my best." He sounded as if he were on mile twenty-six of a marathon.

Moments later she had his full concentration again. He moved his hand over her abdomen, then lower, sliding one finger inside her. She'd anticipated the touch but not the reaction, as if a bolt of electricity had zapped her into another dimension. She pulled her heels high on the bed, nearly shattering with the power of it.

Then he shifted, taking his weight on his forearms, and entered her—slow, smooth, steady.

He stroked once, gently, letting her grow accustomed to him, then followed up with a hard thrust. His technique was flawless, delivering the maximum amount of attention until that pleasure was too much to take. Release exploded, creating a shuddering wave, and he held her until it had rolled all the way through her.

Then he began to move again, once, twice and third time was the charm. He groaned and his body grew tense, then trembled as spasms of satisfaction exploded through him. And she held him close as feelings of exquisite tenderness welled inside her.

She couldn't move and dozed in his arms until he nudged her awake, vowing that he'd been in too big a hurry before, but this time it would be slower. It was until it wasn't and neither of them could wait, but the thrill was no less than before.

And somewhere in the middle of the night he made love to her again. It was without a doubt the best night of her life, and she promised herself that she'd hang on to the glow as long as possible because when morning came she would surely have regrets.

Chapter Ten

Cabot woke before dawn as usual, but having a soft, curvy, warm woman in his arms was definitely a different way to start out the day. And it was a little unsettling because of how easy it would be to get used to waking up like this with Kate every morning. For a short time in his life he'd had that. Then everything had changed.

The thought of going to hell after he died didn't bother him much since he'd spent quite a bit of time there while still on this earth. Putting himself in a situation where it could happen to him again wasn't especially appealing. Although that wouldn't be an issue because Kate's mornings on the ranch were limited to the end of summer.

He tried to move without waking her, but she stirred, then opened her eyes. He saw uncertainty at first. Then it cleared and the realization of where she was along with apparent memories of what they'd done last night made her full lips curve into a smile. His expectation had been that she would regret going to bed with him. He didn't know whether or not to be relieved that she didn't.

"Good morning." He raised up on his elbow.

"Yes, it is." She had the look of a thoroughly satisfied woman.

But he still had to ask. "Are you okay?"

"Fine." Her forehead wrinkled in confusion. "Why?"

"I just get the feeling you don't do that sort of thing, so I wanted to check."

"You were wondering if I'd hate myself in the morning?"

"Well..." He shrugged. "Yes."

"I don't."

"To put a finer point on it...do you hate me?"

"Of course not." She reached out and put a hand on his arm. "I'm a consenting adult and I definitely consented to what we did."

Willing participant was more correct, he thought. "Okay."

"You don't look convinced. Are you thinking this is a rebound move for me?"

"Actually, that hadn't crossed my mind." Mostly because in the heat of the moment he'd lost his mind, what with blood flow diverted to points south of his belt. But he should have considered that. "Now that you mention it, is that what happened?"

Without hesitation she emphatically said, "No. And I'll tell you why I know that."

"I'm listening." For some reason he really wanted to be convinced that she was telling the truth.

"I had nothing to rebound from." She raised up on one elbow, and when the sheet slipped, she pulled it back up to cover her bare breasts.

"Oh?" Cabot forced himself to look into her eyes, even though every ounce of testosterone in his body was coaxing him to look lower.

"I wasn't in love with him."

He remembered her shell-shocked expression in the diner while still wearing the wrinkled wedding gown. The dress she'd put on to get married just a few weeks ago. "How can you be so sure?"

"I know myself, Cabot. There were doubts that I ignored or was too crazy busy to deal with. Once I tried to discuss it with him, but he blew me off and said it was just wedding jitters. Maybe I wanted to believe that, but there's something I'm quite sure of."

"What's that?"

"I didn't miss him. What he did didn't hurt me. If I'd been in love with him, no way would I be here in your bed right now."

"Okay." He believed her and hoped like hell that wouldn't prove to be a mistake.

"In fact," she said, "I think he did me a big favor by cheating on me."

"That needs some explaining. I know men and women process situations differently, but I don't think I could be as philosophical if I caught my fiancée cheating." He was pretty sure about that because there was every indication that his wife had been unfaithful before walking out, and he hadn't been philosophical at all. *Mad as hell* more accurately described his reaction.

Kate's expression was still full of sunshine. "It was a favor because clearly I didn't love him, and the marriage would have been a complicated, messy and costly mistake to undo."

"I know all about that," he said.

That comment took the sun out of her eyes and filled them with questions. "There was just enough passion in your voice to make it sound as if you still have feelings for your wife."

"*Ex*-wife." He shook his head. There was no doubt in his mind that he was over her. And had been for a long time. "The fallout from what happened is something you never forget."

"I see." She glanced at the clock. "I'd better get going. Caroline will be here and ready to cook pretty soon, and she'll need the groceries."

They had just enough time for one more go-around, except his words had efficiently and effectively slammed that door shut. But maybe that was for the best. This thing between them had the potential to be complicated and messy—at least for him. Probably only for him. Which made it *his* problem and character flaw.

"Okay," he finally said.

"I'll go make coffee before I leave."

"That's not necessary."

She shrugged. "It's not a problem."

"Okay, then. Sounds good."

Cabot knew she could find her way around the kitchen without help. So he threw the covers back and walked into the bathroom for a quick shower. Afterward he shaved and combed his hair, then went downstairs, fully expecting her to have left. But she was cooking potatoes, eggs and toast and looking very much at home doing it.

Sliding his arm around her waist and pulling her in for a kiss would feel so natural, and it took every ounce of his willpower to resist the urge.

Instead he said, "You didn't have to go to all this trouble, but it sure smells good."

Apparently her earlier comment about messy, complicated mistakes was forgotten because she slid a sassy look over her shoulder. "Tastes even better than it smells."

His mouth was watering, but it had very little to do with food and a lot to do with her.

Then the phone rang, loud, unexpected and startling. Calls this early weren't unheard of but still unusual, and his first thought was that something had happened to Ty. He grabbed the phone from its charger on the counter and looked at the caller ID. The number wasn't provided, which meant this had nothing to do with his son.

He hit the talk button. "Hello?"

The caller identified himself as a law-enforcement officer from Helena and he was sorry to inform him… Cabot heard the words, but they didn't sink in. This was surreal. He took down a number in case he had further questions, then thanked the officer for letting him know and hung up.

Kate was staring at him. "Who was that, Cabot? You look as if you've seen a ghost."

If he'd been able to manage it, he would have laughed at that. The saying was so close to the truth. He met her gaze and thought how ironic that he'd just been remembering the cheating woman who'd run out on him.

"My ex-wife is dead. She was killed in a car accident last night."

And he had to figure out a way to tell his son that there was now no hope of him ever meeting or having a relationship with his mother.

Kate had regrets about Cabot, but sleeping with him wasn't one of them. She did regret learning that he still had feelings for his ex. He'd denied it, but she'd seen the look in his eyes when he'd told her the news.

It was a very effective way to destroy the

romantic buzz she'd had when she woke up in his bed. A horrible start to the morning after such a magical night.

Because of that, Cabot had been on her mind ever since. Working with the camp kids had distracted her some, but now she was walking to the archery range for her prearranged practice session with Ty and had nothing but time to think. She'd wanted to stay with Cabot earlier, just in case he needed or wanted to talk, but both of them had responsibilities. If there was any good news, it was that Ty's sleepover had allowed his dad some space to collect his thoughts. And Kate was sure there was more to what he was feeling than just concern for his son.

From the compound of camp cabins she followed the dirt path around a curve by the lake and in the distance saw the bales of hay with targets tacked on. It surprised her that a man was standing beside one. The figure looked a lot like Cabot, but Tyler was nowhere in sight. She hadn't seen him by the storage area retrieving his archery equipment, either.

Kate hurried over to her boss and stopped in front of him. The brim of his Stetson shaded his eyes although not his face, but there wasn't much to see. It was wiped clean of emotion.

"Cabot," she said. "What's going on? Is Tyler coming to practice?"

"In a few minutes."

"Have you told him yet…about the phone call?"

He shook his head. "C.J.'s mom brought him home from the sleepover a little while ago. He was anxious to get back to practicing with his bow and arrow after being stuck inside, what with the rain yesterday. I gave him a couple of chores to do when he got home. I wanted to talk to you first."

"So he doesn't know about his mother." She nodded. "Don't worry. I wouldn't have said anything before you got a chance to tell him what happened."

"I didn't think you would. That's not what I was going to say."

If that wasn't it, then what in the world? Another thought came to her. "You don't want me around him." She met his gaze. "I've explained to him that I'm not staying after the summer."

"That's not it, either." For the first time a corner of his mouth quirked up. "You can keep guessing why I'm here if you want. Far be it from me to stifle that fertile imagination of yours, but I'd really like to have this conversation with you before he gets here. And it might be a little quicker if you just let me tell you."

"Okay." More words wanted to come out, but she forced them back.

"I can't decide whether or not to tell him." He rubbed a hand over his neck. "Since you already know about it, I thought—"

"You could use me as a sounding board."

"Yes."

"Anytime you're ready," she encouraged him.

"The thing is, Ty doesn't have any memory of his mother. He's seen pictures of her, but he's only in one of them—she's holding him when he was an infant. On a day-to-day basis, she's had no influence on him whatsoever, good or bad."

"I see."

"If I tell him the news, there's no way it could have a good impact."

Kate figured he was making a case for not saying anything. "What about the emotional ramifications?"

"What do you mean?"

"Well..." She thought carefully about how

to phrase this. "He's talked to me about his friend C.J.'s family, the fact that his mom's husband adopted him."

"And you're interpreting that to mean that he misses his mom?"

"It's hard to miss what you never had. So maybe not *her* exactly, but the idea of having a mom."

Cabot folded his arms over his chest. "Are you saying you think I should tell him?"

"I would never presume to tell you how to raise your son. No one can make that decision but you." When he shifted, the sun hit her in the eyes and she put a hand up to shade them. "But let me play devil's advocate."

"Okay."

"Let's say you keep this information to yourself. What if Ty is somehow holding out hope of his mom coming back? And what if next year, or the year after, or when he's eighteen or twenty-one, he brings up the subject of looking for her? If you don't say anything and he finds out she's been gone for years and you let him believe, by omission, that there was a chance she'd return—" She just looked at him, letting him draw his own conclusions about the consequences.

Cabot's mouth pulled tight for a moment. "Neither of my choices is very good."

"I know." He could turn his son's world upside down now or risk Ty finding out later and lose his trust.

"And she continues to be a thorn in my side—"

That could mean a lot of things, but when Kate felt her chest tighten, it was clear that she was putting a deeply personal spin on the words. It never would affect her one way or the other; she knew that. But she had to ask anyway.

"Were you hoping that she would come back?"

He looked completely disgusted with himself. "A part of me wanted to put the family back together, give Tyler a traditional home."

Was that all about having a family, or did it mean he was still in love with his ex? Again it was none of her business, but what was the harm in asking? He'd get mad? She'd lose his friendship? He'd never kiss her again? Soon she would go back to Los Angeles and wouldn't see him at all, mad or not. And as far as friendship? That shelf life was limited to however many days she had left on the ranch.

So she had very little to lose if she took her curiosity out for a spin. "Cabot, can I ask you a question?"

"What if I say no?"

She shrugged. "I'll ask anyway. You don't have to answer."

"Fair enough."

"Here goes." She blew out a breath. "Were you still in love with your ex-wife?"

"You asked me that earlier."

In his bed. She remembered. "You didn't really give me an answer. Were you?"

Before he could respond, the sound of running feet drifted to them, quickly followed by Ty's voice.

"Kate? Here I come." Excitement and boyish exuberance filled his tone as he rounded the curve.

Cabot's expression turned somewhere in the tortured range when he saw his son. He still hadn't said what he planned to tell the child.

"Hi, Kate. Dad! Are you here to watch me practice?" He had a quiver of arrows on his back and the bow in his hand.

"Ty—" The man took a knee in front of his son.

The little boy frowned. "But what about

the cows you were supposed to move 'cause they ate up all their food? Are they gonna be hungry?"

"No." Cabot smiled. "The other hands can do it without me this one time."

"Because you wanted to see me shoot my bow?"

Kate watched expressions chase across Cabot's face and knew he was reading the same feelings into the boy's words that she was. His son was feeling the downside of being raised by a busy, hardworking single dad.

"I'd really like to see you shoot." He braced a forearm on his knee and met his child's gaze. "But first there's something I have to tell you."

"What?" Ty's anxious tone said he was getting a serious vibe.

Kate was glad Cabot had decided to tell his son, but maybe he wanted to do it alone. "I'll just go back and see if Caroline needs any help."

Cabot glanced up. "If it's all the same to you, Kate, I'd appreciate it if you'd stay."

"All right." She stood a little to the side, giving father and son some space. If there was anything she could do to make this easier, she'd do it in a heartbeat.

"What's wrong, Dad? Am I in trouble?"

"No, son. But I got some news this morning that you have a right to know. It's about your mom."

"The lady in the pictures you showed me?"

"Yes."

"Is she coming to see me?"

As Kate watched Cabot's face, she saw that the slight hope in Ty's voice took a huge toll on the father's heart.

"No, she's not," he said quietly, then reached out and put a big hand on the boy's shoulder. "She was in a car accident. I'm sorry, son, but she was hurt really bad and didn't make it."

Tyler blinked. "She's dead?"

"That's right. I'm really sorry to have to tell you this."

"I know."

Cabot was studying the boy carefully. "This is a lot to take in, buddy. How are you feeling?"

"I'm not sure." He shrugged his thin shoulders. "I guess I thought someday she'd want to see me."

A muscle jerked in Cabot's jaw. "It's natural you'd feel that way."

"Now she never can." The boy's tone was wistful but not miserable.

"No, she can't."

"Daddy, am I s'posed to be sad?"

"Is that how you feel?" Cabot asked.

"Maybe." Ty shrugged. "A little, I guess. But not too much. Is that bad?"

"No, buddy. Whatever you're feeling is just fine. There's no right or wrong about it."

"Okay."

He gently pulled the boy into his arms. "I love you, son."

"I love you, too, Dad."

Tyler stepped away, a thoughtful expression scrunching up his face. "Do I have to go home?"

"You can if you want." Cabot stood and ruffled his son's hair. "Is there something else you want to do?"

"I'd really like to practice with Kate." He glanced at her, then back to his dad. "And it would be cool if you stayed to watch."

Cabot smiled down at his son. "Then that's what we'll do."

"Cool."

Tyler chattered to his father about nocking

an arrow, the best stance for a beginner and how he needed to buy a guard so the bow-string snapping his arm wouldn't hurt. Then he took his mark and started shooting one arrow after another, most of them hitting the target circle, although no bull's-eye yet.

Cabot stood to the side, watching, encouraging, approving. And talking to Kate in between.

"That went well," she said in a voice low enough that Ty couldn't hear. "You were so good with him."

"Didn't feel that way."

She understood that. How was there anything good about telling your child he would never get a chance to meet his mother? But the patience, sensitivity and concern this man had shown were pretty awesome. "It was the right thing to do. Telling him, I mean."

"It doesn't feel right, either." Anger swirled in his eyes. "There's nothing right about what she did. She left him twice. Once by walking out and then by dying."

It was time to change the subject. "So, what do you think about your son's skill with the bow and arrow?"

"He's really come a long way." He smiled over at the boy, who was busy retrieving the arrows and replenishing his quiver. "You must be a pretty good teacher."

"Don't sound so surprised."

"Seriously?" He grinned. "I saw you on that magazine cover in a bathing suit, holding a fishing rod."

"Don't let the bikini fool you. I was in that magazine because I conduct seminars on survival techniques."

"Everyone in town is talking about the cover girl in our midst. You know Caroline knows the truth about you, too."

"She does. Nolan told her," Kate confirmed. "We talked about it this morning."

"I talked to her, too," he said. "And she thinks you should expand the camp-survival class we already have and teach it."

Kate could not describe how exhilarating the feeling of being good at something, and getting recognized for it, felt. She wanted to hug him and just barely managed to hold back. "I'd love that. Sounds like a plan."

It was probably good to have a plan, and someday soon Kate needed to get one. For goodness' sake, she'd slept with the man. That was not something she did lightly. She wasn't a one-night-stand kind of girl, which meant she was developing feelings for him.

For so many reasons she shouldn't be, not the least of which was that he might still care about a woman who had treated him and their child badly. Sydney had said anger and love were flip sides of the same coin, and Cabot was clearly furious at Ty's mother for her double abandonment.

Cabot might mourn the loss of hope in reuniting his family. But Kate mourned the loss of any chance to tell that woman off, to say to her face that she was a terrible person for throwing away her beautiful son and a good man.

Kate had run from a man who wasn't even in the same league as Cabot. If she didn't stop herself, she could end up falling for the rancher. And leaving Blackwater Lake would be a lot more traumatic than what she'd been through just before she'd arrived.

Chapter Eleven

Cabot sat in the dining-room-turned-classroom and watched Kate teach a group of twelve kids basic survival skills. Not only did she seem to know her stuff, but also she looked really good up there talking about it. Hard to believe the summer was already more than half over. It had been an eventful one, including getting closure with his ex. In the past two weeks he'd been watching his son carefully, looking for emotional aftereffects from the news about his mother's passing. Ty didn't seem to have any issues.

Cabot was glad he'd told the boy everything and also grateful for Kate being a sounding board and gentle presence when he broke the news. With the archery range close by, Ty had an activity to distract him. And the kid was getting pretty darn good with a bow and arrow.

What pleased Cabot most was Kate saying how well he'd handled the situation. He hadn't known her long, but in all that time he'd never seen her hold back, whether her opinion was good or bad. So he took her words as a compliment.

She was standing in the front of the room with a dry-erase board propped on a chair. He'd come in quietly after her presentation started and sat off to the side and near the door, a place where he could observe her and see kids' expressions to determine if they were understanding the material presented. As far as he could tell, no one had noticed his entrance. The kids in attendance ranged in age from nine to thirteen and were mesmerized by what Kate had to share. This class was mandatory for any child signed up for the overnight campout, but Kate had expanded the basic program and Cabot wanted to monitor the new material.

"Before hiking or walking an area, always do your research," she was saying. "Know your surroundings. Learning about local plants and animals could save your life."

A blond boy raised his hand and said, "How?"

"Food. So you know which berries are safe to eat, for instance."

"What about animals?" This was from another boy, a redheaded, freckle-faced kid who looked as though he could stir up mischief without a firm hand to rein him in. "Or bugs."

Kate's expression didn't change. She must've known that he wanted a creeped-out-girl reaction and wasn't going to give him one. "They can be a good source of protein. I hope it never happens, but if you get hungry enough, you'll be grateful for that grasshopper."

"Ew." This was a collective reaction from the rest of the kids in the room.

Kate grinned. "Okay, listen up and you won't get lost in the woods long enough to have to eat bugs." She looked around. "Now, then, always make sure to tell someone where you're going and how long you'll be gone."

"That's what my mom always says," the redheaded boy chimed in.

"Parents know best. It would be a good idea to pay attention to them, Aaron." She looked at Ty and sympathy lurked in her eyes. "Next, remember to bring a cell phone or CB radio, some communication device in case you're lost or injured. Bring survival gear like a knife, matches in a waterproof container, a whistle, signal mirror."

When she met his gaze, Cabot knew she'd seen him come in and was now remembering the night she told him about how to make a fire without matches. By using a condom. He smiled to himself, thinking how much he preferred using it the way they had the night of the rainstorm. That had been a couple of weeks ago, and there'd been no opportunity to get her alone since. Not for lack of wanting to.

His gaze dropped to her tanned legs, beautifully showcased in her denim shorts. Memories of them wrapped around his waist kept him awake nights. The rest of her was equally as tantalizing. This wasn't the first time in his life he'd been relieved no one could read his mind, but it was quite possibly the most inappropriate setting for what he was thinking. A lot of kids were in this room, including his own son.

"All of those things are what you should have if your day in the woods is planned.

Now we're going to talk about what to do if you lose sight of the group."

"Like if you're the last in line and everyone else in your family walks away?" The little dark-haired girl's voice shook a little.

"That's right, Gina." Kate walked over and squatted beside her. Obviously she'd heard the anxiety, too. "Did that happen to you?"

Gina nodded solemnly. "I stopped to look at a flower and they kept going. Then I couldn't hear them anymore."

"That must have been scary." She put her hand on the little girl's arm. "What did you do?"

"I bet she started to cry," Aaron said.

Kate looked at him, anger briefly flashing in her eyes, but when she responded, her voice was calm and even. "Crying when you're sad or scared is a perfectly normal reaction for anyone."

"I did cry a little," Gina admitted, giving the boy a blistering look. "But I just stayed still and they came back for me."

"That was exactly the right thing to do." Kate stood and walked back to the front of the room, then took a stack of papers from the chair. She handed them to his son. "Would you pass these out for me, Ty?"

"Sure." He hopped up and smiled at her as if he thought she hung the moon.

Cabot was starting to feel that way, too, but he was doing his darnedest to fight it.

"Hi, Dad. I didn't know you were here." Tyler gave him a toothy grin and handed him a paper.

"Thanks, son. I slipped in after Kate started and didn't want to interrupt."

"It's really good," his son said. "I gotta finish handing out papers. Are you gonna stay till it's over?"

He hadn't planned to, but the eager expression in the boy's eyes changed his mind. That and the opportunity to just watch Kate. "Yeah, I'll be here."

"Cool." Ty made sure everyone in class had the handout.

Kate wrote a word on the dry-erase board and underlined it. "The number one thing to do when you're lost is STOP."

"Why is it capitalized?" Gina asked.

"So you can remember. *S*—sit down. *T*—think. *O*—observe. *P*—prepare for survival by gathering materials."

"Like what?" Aaron sat up in his seat and actually looked interested.

"Rocks to make a circle for a fire. Dry

twigs to burn. Tree branches for a shelter. Berries just in case you get hungry." She looked around, waiting for questions, and when there weren't any, she continued. "You need to orient yourself. First use a piece of brightly colored clothing or a pile of leaves to mark your location. Then figure out your directions—north, south, east, west."

"How?" Ty asked.

"We all know the sun rises in the east and sets in the west. If it's late afternoon and the sun is on your right, you're facing south." She assessed their expressions and figured, as he did, that they didn't quite get that. "Don't worry. We'll practice."

"Then what do you do?" Aaron wanted to know.

"Stay in one place. This increases your chances of being found and reduces the amount of energy your body uses. That means you won't need as much water and food to keep you going."

Interesting stuff, Cabot thought. He took all of this for granted because he'd grown up with land all around and spent time in the wilderness with his father. At the time it felt like a lecture, but now that he had a son, he was grateful for everything he'd been taught.

Unlike his father, Kate was patient and much more fun to watch. She seemed to keep the kids' attention even as she gave them practical information.

"If it's hot out, find shade. And, boys, don't be tempted to take off your shirts."

"How come?" Ty asked.

"You can easily become dehydrated and sunburned."

Cabot got a mental image of Kate in that bathing suit on the magazine cover. If they were alone, he sure wouldn't mind seeing her in that bikini for real—and then take it off her in the shade. And if he didn't STOP, he was going to have to give himself a time-out.

Almost as if she could read his thoughts, Kate took the pen and wrote *Fire* on the board. "Another way to prepare is to start a fire. We'll do a whole class just on safely doing that."

"Cool," Aaron said.

"No—hot," Ty countered, looking pleased with himself when Gina laughed.

"Signal your location," Kate continued. "Make noise—whistle, shout, sing, bang rocks together. If you're in an open area visible from the air, make something searchers can see." She drew a triangle, then wrote *SOS* inside it. "Do something like this in a sandy area or use leaves and tree branches."

Cabot could see the kids were shifting in their seats and looking around, getting restless. At this point they wouldn't retain anything.

"What do you say we call it a day?" Kate apparently had noticed, too. "We'll go over the rest of the material tomorrow. I think it's getting close to lunchtime."

The kids nodded and stood. Aaron started toward the door with Gina. "I wonder if bugs are on the menu."

"Gross," she said, wrinkling her nose.

"How about caterpillars?"

Kate heard and walked over to him. "Never eat brightly colored bugs. And always cook them to get germs off. Grasshoppers are okay. They're quite good, actually."

Gina had hurried out the door ahead of him and didn't hear the remark, but Aaron sure did. He didn't say "ew," but Cabot would swear he turned just a little green.

He and Ty moved to the front of the room and Kate joined them there. Cabot tipped his hat to her. "Nicely done, Miss Scott."

"Which part? The information? Or the bug-cuisine part at the end?" She used a rag to wipe off the board.

"Both."

"Did you really eat a grasshopper?" Tyler asked skeptically.

"Yes."

"Really?" Cabot asked.

"I wouldn't lie." She made a cross over her heart. "In the grown-up version of this class, you have to eat a bug to pass."

"Then I think I'd get an F," Ty said. "Gina's right. That's gross."

"Was it?" Cabot asked. "Gross, I mean?"

"Let's just say that if you're really hungry, it's better than nothing."

"So, and I quote, listen carefully and never get lost in the woods long enough to have to eat bugs."

She laughed. "I'm glad to know someone was paying attention."

He had been when he hadn't been having fantasies about her shapely legs wrapped around his waist.

"I was listening," Ty said. "But if you were there, you could just tell me what to do."

"If I was where?" she asked.

"The campout. Are you going?" He was looking up at her hopefully.

"No one has said anything to me about it." She glanced at Cabot. "I just took over the survival basics from one of the other counselors."

"My dad takes the kids who sign up for it in advance," Ty explained. He looked at his father as something occurred to him. "You never come to camp activities except for that. How come you're here today?"

Cabot almost winced. He knew his son wasn't being critical, just making an observation and asking for an explanation about the change. But it made him think. Maybe he should show up more. Not because he had news about his son's mother or to keep an eye on a new teacher.

"I wanted to see how Kate's new class on wilderness training went." Mostly.

"It was good." Tyler nodded emphatically. "I liked the bug stuff."

And maybe he has a little crush on Gina, Cabot thought. Wasn't it too soon for all of that? He wasn't looking forward to navigating his son's teenage years by himself. But you played the hand you were dealt.

"I'm glad you enjoyed the lesson." Kate smiled at the boy.

"Dad, I have an idea."

"I thought I smelled smoke," Cabot teased. "But that was you using your head."

Ty rolled his eyes. "Kate should go with us on the campout."

"Not as the cook." He met her gaze and saw her grin.

"Don't knock it till you've tried it."

"It's really fun, Kate," the boy persisted, looking up at Cabot. "Please say it's okay for her to go with us."

Obviously it meant a lot to his son. Cabot wouldn't mind, either. She was good with kids and good company. But it wasn't part of her job and she probably wouldn't want to rough it.

"You don't have to," he said. "But there's always room for one more, and an extra pair of eyes on the kids is always welcome. You can do hands-on instruction on the trail about edible plants and animals."

"If you're sure about this, I'd like very much to go."

"Yay," Ty said. "I'm going to tell the other kids that Kate is coming with us on the campout." He ran out of the dining room.

"You know you can't bring that fishing rod. The one you were holding on that magazine cover. Hiking in means traveling light."

"I left it at home anyway."

Was she blushing? he wondered. The next question was why she would be. Millions of people probably saw her in that bikini, but she was blushing for him. Which kind of made him feel good.

But Cabot wasn't at all sure this was a "yay" sort of deal. It could very well be a bad idea.

Kate gathered up pencils and paper in the dining room so that tables would be cleared and set up for the lunch crowd. To her surprise, Cabot stuck around to help her. He'd watched her closely during the presentation, which was both intimidating and thrilling. She'd given talks to outdoor enthusiasts lots of times, but there'd never been a man in the audience whom she'd been to bed with.

"Where does this go?" he asked, pointing to the dry-erase board. "In the equipment shed?"

She nodded. "I can get that. It's not heavy. You must have more important things to do."

"Not just now. I'll give you a hand." He picked it up and headed toward the door where the kids had exited moments before. "You have a shed key?"

"Yes. All the counselors do." She followed him out onto the porch.

At the bottom of the stairs, Aaron, Ty and Gina were standing around talking. The red-headed boy said, "The sun is almost straight up in the sky. How can we tell which way is south?"

"Kate said she would show us," Gina answered.

"Better not get lost before she does," Ty told him. "It's pretty scary when you don't know which way to go."

"If you were listening," the other boy retorted good-naturedly, "you would know that it's best not to go anywhere if you're lost."

"STOP." Ty held up his fingers to count off the letters. "Sit down. Think. Observe. Prepare."

Standing in the shadowy doorway where the kids didn't notice them, Kate glanced up at Cabot. He looked impressed and very proud of his son.

"What if you can't find any food right where you are?" Gina wondered.

"Mark your spot and keep it in sight so you can move around a little and hunt," Aaron told her.

"I didn't think that kid was listening," Cabot whispered.

"Neither did I. But good for him."

Gina said, "We should find a bug and cook it."

"I thought that grossed you out." Aaron raised his eyebrows. "Why should we do that?"

"To eat it," Ty said.

"I dare you to eat it," the other boy shot back.

"It won't kill you," Gina told him. "Kate said so."

Cabot leaned down and said quietly, "Apparently your word is gospel."

The feel of his breath on her ear raised shivers that raced down her arms. Her voice was a little ragged when she answered, "Before they strike out on their own, we better schedule a follow-up class quickly to clue them in on what is and isn't edible."

"Yeah." Cabot moved out of the doorway and down the steps, stopping beside the trio.

"Hi, Dad," Ty said, spotting him. "Hey, Kate. We want to build a fire without matches and catch a bug to cook it."

"Hmm." Laughter sparkled in her eyes, but she managed to stay as serious as the kids. "It is almost lunchtime. If you're too hungry to wait, you could do that. But remember, bugs might spoil your appetite. And Caroline is making mac and cheese."

Aaron looked relieved to have an out that would allow him to save face. "Maybe we can do it on the campout."

"Are you going?" Gina asked Aaron.

"Yeah."

"Me, too," Ty piped up. "And Kate is. You can show us then, right?"

"If you're still interested," she answered.

"Let's go skip rocks on the lake until lunch is ready," Ty suggested.

"Okay." Gina looked at him. "Can you show me how again?"

"Sure. Aaron's really good at it, too. We'll both help you." He looked up at Kate. "Is that okay?"

She could see from where she stood that there was a counselor with a group of kids by the water. They would be supervised. "Sure."

"'Bye, Kate. Last one there is a rotten egg. See you later, Dad."

Before Cabot could answer, the three were racing away to see who could reach the lake first.

"What I wouldn't give to have that much energy," Kate commented.

"I know what you mean." He looked down at her, admiration in his gaze. "You did a good job communicating that information to them."

"I'm glad you think so." Maybe her preoccupation with him hadn't thrown her off as much as she'd feared.

"As you know, it's required for the kids signed up for the campout, but you made it fun and interesting even for the ones who are staying behind. You really had their attention."

That reminded her. Ty had been transparent in his eagerness for her to go along on the campout. She needed to talk to Cabot about his son. But first they had to stow the board and other supplies.

"We should put that away," she told him.

He nodded and they walked around the building to the equipment shed. She reached into the pocket of her denim shorts to get the key and unlocked the dead bolt. She flipped the light switch just inside the door.

The windowless space was well organized with an area for office supplies to the right. Bins held soccer balls, basketballs and footballs. Hooks on the wall held bows and quivers of arrows. Paddleboards stood upright to the left. The equipment was kept under lock and key because kids were unpredictable. You didn't know when they might take it into their head to try something. This way they needed permission.

"The board goes over there with the office supplies," she told him. "Just stand it against the wall beside the shelf with the computer paper."

Cabot did as requested and they turned off the light, then locked up the shed.

Kate shoved the key back in her pocket and turned to find Cabot standing just behind her with a funny look on his face.

"What's wrong?" She brushed a hand down her ponytail. "Is there a spider in my hair?"

"Are you afraid of spiders?"

"Of course. Anyone in their right mind is afraid of them." She shuddered. "To quote every girl in that room, 'ew.'"

He laughed. "So all that about catching and eating bugs is just talk?"

"You did notice that I kept stressing that it's only as a last resort?"

"Yeah. But I think the kids are really intrigued by the thought of doing it."

She nodded. "But I'm really hoping they forget about eating bugs by the time we go on the campout."

The "we" part of that sentence reminded her why she was now included and what she wanted to say. "Cabot, I need to ask you something."

"Okay." He slid his fingertips into the pockets of his worn jeans. "Shoot."

"Have you talked with Ty? About me, I mean? And not getting attached?"

"Not yet."

"I didn't think so." It was important that he understood why she was asking. "I reminded him that I won't be staying. But a little bit ago when he asked me to go along on the camping trip, I got the feeling it hasn't sunk in for him just yet."

"I saw that," he admitted. "And I think you're right."

She had hoped to be wrong, but the man was Ty's father and he'd noticed, too. "I think he needs to hear from both of us, especially you, that you and I will never be romantically involved."

"I know." His mouth pulled into a grim line. "But I just had to break the news about his mother. It seemed like waiting a little longer was a good idea."

She nodded. "The reality of losing her for good could be part of the reason he's still pushing me at you. On some level he feels that loss and wants to replace her."

"Maybe. I'm no shrink, but getting this out in the open is probably a good idea. Warning and preparation are both important. I know how it feels to be abandoned. And to be blindsided by it."

"Because of what your wife did to you."

"She's not the only one. My mother did the same thing when I was a little older than Ty."

"Oh, Cabot..." Kate simply stared at him. She couldn't believe this man had been left twice. No wonder he was so guarded. "That's awful. I'm so sorry."

"I'm over what happened, but I do know how it feels to be left behind." If possible, he looked even more grim. "I got through it by being angry. But my dad never got to that point. He never stopped loving her, making excuses for her behavior."

"And waiting for her to come home."

He nodded. "Until the day he died, at the sound of a car door unexpectedly closing, I saw hope live and die in his eyes. I'm pretty sure that didn't do anything good for his health." He shrugged. "One day his heart just gave out."

Kate read between the lines. As far as she knew, it wasn't even a medically approved cause of death, but she would bet that his father had died of a broken heart. And being the good son that he was, Cabot had taken over the ranch even though he'd been considering another career. So a woman's rejection had led to a turning point that had totally changed the course of his life. That would leave a mark on anyone—inside, where no one could see it.

"I'm really sorry, Cabot." What else could she say? "But not all women do that."

"Couldn't prove it by me." He met her gaze. "But I'll have that talk with Tyler and make sure he understands that you're not staying."

"Okay. Thanks. It would ease my mind because I'd never do anything to hurt him."

He nodded, lifted his hand in farewell and walked away without a word. That silence spoke volumes. He didn't trust her even though he'd known from the beginning that she wasn't staying. It was only ever going to be a summer job. Still, she couldn't blame him for protecting himself. What he'd just told her underscored his deep resistance to commitment.

He was dedicated to his son, but everyone else in his life was only provisional. He rescued people because it was safe and didn't put his emotional well-being at risk. But that begged the question—why had he slept with her?

The only answer she could come up with was that he'd done it because she was leaving and nothing could come of it. For him, even the most superficial relationship came with safeguards and conditions. Attraction had been simmering between them since the day they'd met, but he wouldn't let himself act on it until he learned she didn't need rescuing. And the only reason he'd let down his guard then was because she was temporary.

But what if she wasn't? She would give almost anything to be able to stick around permanently, just to see how he would handle her presence. See if he would run.

Chapter Twelve

Three days after giving her talk on wilderness survival, a couple of workshops on starting a fire safely and identifying edible forest plants, Kate followed Cabot into the woods with six children and camp counselor Diane Castillo, making it two children per adult. The whole merry band had just arrived at a clearing by the lake. Logs had been arranged in a square with a circular black scorched spot in the center where previous fires had burned. It was weird being off the trail; she'd been following her boss's broad shoulders for several hours and would miss the view now that they were stopped.

"This is a good spot." Cabot slid his heavy pack from said shoulders and set it on the hard-packed dirt in the open area away from the trees and a short distance from the edge of the lake.

Aaron, Gina and Ty were there with three other kids from the camp—David, Samantha and Rob. All of them looked around, their eyes widening with excitement.

All except Ty. He set his lighter pack down beside his father's. "We always camp here, Dad."

"Because it's a good spot."

"What makes it a good spot?" David was about twelve and wore wire-rimmed glasses—very Harry Potter. He'd never been on an overnight campout before. "Shouldn't we be under the trees? For cover?"

"Not a good idea for two reasons." Cabot helped the boy slide off his pack. "Number one, this is a safe place to build a fire. There's no nearby brush, bushes or trees to catch fire if a breeze suddenly kicks up. Number two, we won't damage a fragile ecosystem on this hard, rocky ground."

"Cool," David said, taking in the terrain around them.

"Any more questions?" Cabot asked.

Samantha, a quiet little brown-haired girl, raised her hand. "Why did you pick up trash when we were walking here?"

"I should have explained that while we were on the trail, but I wanted to make sure we got here in plenty of time to set up camp and have some fun."

"I can tell her, Dad," Ty volunteered. At a nod from his father he continued. "We need to leave everything in the woods the way we found it. Take only pictures, leave only footprints. That means don't do anything that harms the earth or the animals."

"That's right." Cabot ruffled the boy's hair. "Potato-chip bags, aluminum cans and other paper don't occur in nature."

"When we find it," Ty added, "we pick it up for someone else who forgot to or doesn't know any better."

"If we take care of the land, it will take care of us," his father added.

Kate smiled. Ty had been well trained by a man who had a soul-deep connection to the land that had been in his family for generations. He was already training his replacement for the family's ranching business and other interests, not just by what he said but by everything he did. This might have been

Cabot's plan B as far as a career path, but he was awfully good at it. Whether he would admit the obvious or not, this life was in his soul.

"Okay, we have some work to do."

As Cabot was assigning two kids to each adult, Ty insisted on being paired with Kate. She met his father's gaze and knew there'd been no father-son chat yet. Now certainly wasn't the time for it, and selfishly she was glad. Ty was a great kid and she sincerely enjoyed hanging out with him.

They broke into groups and set up tents, gathered rocks for a fire pit and arranged dry wood inside it for later. They positioned provisions in an area not too far from where the cooking would be done, and everyone refilled their water containers. Now it was time to have fun.

"Who wants to go fishing?" Cabot asked.

"We don't have fishing poles. They were too bulky to bring with us," Aaron reminded him. All the kids had been instructed about what to pack and what not to.

"I can take care of that." Cabot grinned at their clueless expressions. "Let's go."

Kate smiled as the children eagerly followed him without question. The trust in him was obvious. Kate could understand that. She trusted him, too, which seemed odd after her fiancé's betrayal, but it was a fact.

Cabot showed them how to find a long stick and tie a piece of string to the end of it with a hook attached. From his backpack he'd also taken a container of bait. Aaron did his best to be macho, but in the end Cabot patiently put a worm on the boy's hook. He was there to help whoever needed it. The other boys didn't and looked awfully superior about it.

Kate knew that would just get worse when they grew into men and were smack in the middle of learning about girls. How she wished it would be possible for her to watch Ty grow up, evolve into the heartbreaker he showed signs of becoming. Girls were going to love him, and he would return the favor. If his father's experiences didn't taint the boy's attitude about dating.

As Cabot led the group down to the lake's edge, Kate expected any second to hear a rousing rendition of "Heigh-ho, heigh-ho, it's off to work we go." Diane stood beside her, observing everything. She was black-haired, olive-skinned and in her early twenties. A single teacher who lived locally, she taught at Blackwater Lake Elementary School. She'd been working at the summer camp even before graduating from college and starting her teaching career.

"I've never seen him quite this involved before."

"Who? Cabot?"

Diane nodded. "It's interesting."

"Doesn't he always come along for this outing?"

"Yes." The other counselor met her gaze. "And he's always good with the kids. Patient, but distant. Something's different about him. As if his mind isn't somewhere else, distracted by a dozen different things. He's really in the moment."

"How do you mean?"

"I guess it always felt as if he was just going through the motions because Tyler wanted him here." Diane shaded her eyes with her hand and watched Cabot talking to the children by the lake. "Today he's really taking his time with the kids."

"It's obvious that he cares deeply about the environment."

"Yes, he does." Diane looked at her. "But I'm not sure it's only about the environment."

Kate's heart stuttered and she wondered

about the meaning of those words. "You're not talking about me."

"What do you think?" She shrugged. "He looks at you a lot when he thinks no one is watching him."

"You're imagining it." Kate wasn't sure whether she wanted the statement confirmed or denied.

"I don't think I am." The other counselor met her gaze. "I've been working summer camp for six years. Female counselors have come and gone. I've seen him socialize in town and at church, talking to women, both locals and tourists."

"What's your point?"

"I've never seen him look at anyone the way he looks at you."

That was flattering and disconcerting in equal parts. But Kate wondered if Diane had ever seen him look at his wife. "It's probably just because he thought I was a flake who ran away from her wedding."

"That could be why he looks angry about it, but I'd say the expression on his face is more about what he wants."

If Cabot was that transparent, Kate figured her face and feelings were like an open book. Protesting would only lend weight to what the other woman had said and there was no point to that. She and Cabot had acknowledged the attraction and also their understanding that it would end soon.

She looked at the other woman and said, "I honestly don't know what to say to that."

"I understand. And I'm sorry. It was inappropriate to bring it up. I just feel protective of him. And I'm surly today." Diane sighed. "You know, I should go down there and help supervise the kids, but I'd sure love to put my feet up for a few minutes. I hate to play this card, but I've got my period and the cramps are killing me after the hike."

"I can go." Did she sound too eager? Kate wondered.

"Would you mind?"

"Of course not." It was scary how much she didn't mind. Being with Cabot made her happy. And what was the harm in enjoying the feeling while she could?

Kate walked down the slight bank and stopped beside Cabot. "Need any help?"

When he glanced down, something smoldered in his eyes. "Everything is quiet right now, but if anyone actually catches anything, it could get exciting."

"And if they don't, you know someone is going to ask about eating bugs."

"I wish I didn't have pasta in my backpack as an alternative because I'd really like to see you herd grasshoppers." He grinned. "It would be even more interesting to see you cook up a batch."

"That's not my best event. I'd much rather clean fish."

"Have you ever done that before?"

"Do bears poop in the woods?" She laughed at his pained expression. "Companies pay me to advertise their products, which requires me to be competent while engaging in outdoor activities, including but not limited to catching and cleaning fish."

"So that rod you were holding on the cover of that magazine wasn't just a prop?" Again his eyes darkened with intensity.

It seemed to her that they'd been over that already, but whatever. "As difficult as it might be to believe, I actually know what to do with it. And don't look so surprised."

"Can't help it. I find myself unable to picture you putting a worm on a hook or gutting a trout."

"Why?" She wasn't asking because she was annoyed. Being underestimated had happened all her life. In his case, for some reason she just wanted Cabot to say the words out loud, right here in the outdoors.

He shifted uncomfortably. “All right. I admit it’s tough to imagine you doing it because of the way you look.”

“How do I look?”

“You know.”

“Not really.” She shrugged. “I have no idea what you mean.”

“I’ll spell it out for you. You’re so beautiful it’s hard to picture you grimy and wet and smelling like fish. Go ahead. Call me a chauvinist, opinionated, closed-minded pig.”

“I don’t have to. You just did that for me.” She laughed, pleased beyond words that he thought she was pretty. “Seriously, is it such a stretch that I could be capable in the outdoors? Or that I love it?”

“Yes.” He met her gaze with a stubborn, determined set to his mouth.

Kate was sorry she’d made him say it because she got more than she’d bargained for. The truth was he didn’t want to believe she could embrace the wide-open spaces because that was his world and would give him a reason not to let her into it. He’d made that mistake with his wife and wouldn't make the same one again.

Funny how differently they responded in this situation. He was counting on her crumbling under the pressure and inconveniences of being in the wilderness, but his deep respect for the land had only made her like him more. Because her family had moved often, she'd never felt connected anywhere. Until now. The first time she'd seen Blackwater Lake—the town, mountains and lake itself—she'd fallen in love with it. After spending time here, nothing about that had changed.

She wasn't anything like the woman who'd walked out on Cabot, the one he still had feelings for.

The shame of it was that if he could let go, Kate had a feeling they could have something special. But that was impossible because he was still holding on to the past with both hands.

Normally when Cabot was sitting with a tin cup of coffee between his hands out under the stars by a campfire, he felt completely at peace, but not tonight. The kids had been bunked down for about an hour. David and Rob shared a tent. Gina and Samantha had paired off in another. Ty was with Aaron. When they'd given the flashlights-out order, there'd been a lot of hollering back and forth, but that had faded to quiet conversation. He'd expected the girls to go on the longest, but his son held that record. Now all was quiet.

The two female counselors were in the last tent and he had one to himself. That was the source of his restlessness. He was wishing pretty hard he was sharing a tent with Kate. But that wasn't possible and no amount of stargazing or fire-watching could change what was.

She was really something. He knew no one had named that terrible hurricane after her, but it would be fitting. Katrina Scott had blown into town wearing a white gown she hadn't gotten married in and proceeded to turn his life upside down.

He was certain she'd been bluffing when she'd looked him in the eye and challenged him to donate her paycheck to his favorite charity. But she'd been telling the truth, and he wasn't sure whether or not that was a good thing. She had a life and didn't really need his help. That should have been a relief, but it bothered him and he wasn't sure why.

The dying embers kept the tin pot of coffee warm. He reached over and lifted it out to fill his cup. Caffeine wouldn't keep him awake, but thoughts of Kate sure would. She was so near yet completely out of his reach.

That was when he heard movement behind him from Kate's tent. He had a better-than-even chance it wasn't Diane because his luck just didn't run that good.

"Is this log taken?"

Kate's hushed voice tied his gut in a knot. He struggled with the stupid happy feelings pouring through him and tamped down the urge to pull her into his lap.

"I guess I can share." He slid sideways. "I thought everyone was asleep."

"Everyone but you and me." She rubbed her hands together and held them toward what was left of the fire. "Are you standing guard to make sure the fire is out? In the wilderness-survival rules, it says someone has to watch for forty-five minutes in case there's wind and sparks that could compromise nearby trees and brush."

"Rules were meant to be broken." In addition to the faint glow of the dying embers, a propane lantern illuminated the clearing. He could see the teasing laughter in her eyes. "I'm pretty sure if I douse what's left of this fire with what's left of the coffee, then stir that up to smother any sparks, it will be enough to keep the wilderness safe and only take about thirty seconds." His mouth quirked up. "Or maybe I'll get wild and throw dirt on it for good measure."

"Oh, no." She faked a horrified look, then laughed. "Knock yourself out."

"How come you're still awake?" He'd hoped for a neutral tone, but it was ragged with what he recognized as longing.

"Couldn't sleep," she answered.

"Not even after that hike?"

"Nope. You know how sometimes it's a challenge to shut your mind off?"

Sadly, he did. Maybe she'd caught it from him, and by that he meant he had a bad feeling that he was on her mind just like she was on his. But that thought was going to stay safely in his head.

He changed the subject. "Nice night."

"Beautiful." She sighed. "I've spent a lot of time outdoors, and this is one of the prettiest spots I've ever seen. Thanks for letting me come along."

"It was Ty's idea," he reminded her. "But I'm glad you like it."

"I do. And, it has to be said, you are very impressive, sir."

"I'm glad you think so," he said, "but I can't say I know why you do."

"Oh, just teaching the kids about respecting nature. Leaving the land the way they found it. And you showed them by example that it's still possible to have fun."

"You think they did?"

"Absolutely." She shifted and their shoulders brushed.

Talk about sparks, he thought. No one could see them, but he sure as heck felt them all over just from that small touch. And he had on a denim jacket. This wasn't good at all.

"So," he said, "you're pretty impressive, too. Nice job cooking that trout Tyler caught."

"I'm glad someone liked it. The kids sure turned up their noses, but at least they tried."

"It was delicious, in my opinion. But I've learned that mac and cheese goes over better than fish when you're talking about what kids will eat." When she didn't respond, he glanced over and saw that she was looking pensive. "What's wrong?"

"Nothing. It's just—" She caught the bottom corner of her lip between her teeth. "You seemed to enjoy yourself today, too."

"I did."

"Diane said that's a change."

He thought for a moment about past outings and realized the other counselor had known him a long time and would see differences. Finally he said, "Maybe."

The way Kate was looking right now told him that the counselor had said more than that. Kate's husky voice was inviting him to confirm, deny or explain.

He didn't want to do any of the above, even though Diane was right about him. He hadn't been aware that his attitude showed, but today was the most fun he'd ever had on one of these campouts.

In fact, he'd spent a lot more time hanging out with the camp kids in general this summer, and that was all about Kate. A subconscious need to see her had him visiting the activities more often and reminded him how much he enjoyed interacting with the campers. He'd wanted more kids of his own before that option left along with his wife. That taught him a man couldn't count on a relationship being solid and, without a guarantee, he wouldn't be responsible for more kids growing up in a single-parent home.

Kate rubbed her hands together again.

"Are you cold?" He was only too happy to change the subject.

"No. It's chilly, but my sweatshirt is fine." She folded her arms across her middle. "Should we be worried that the kids high-fived about not taking showers?"

"They're okay until tomorrow." He chuckled. "It's just one night. They're kids. I'm pretty sure none of them will need therapy."

"Good. Just saying..." She laughed, then rested her head on his shoulder.

It felt good—too good. Made him ache to put his arm around her, hold her hand, do those intimate things a man did with a woman he cared about. He couldn't say anything without his voice giving all of that away, so he let the silence stretch out between them.

Finally she said, "I can't believe how fast this summer has gone."

When it was over she'd leave. She didn't say that, but Cabot could read between the lines. "Yeah, it did go fast."

She sat up straight, turning off the intimacy. "When you said it was Ty's idea for me to come along—"

"I know. I'm sorry I haven't talked to him yet. I will when we get back tomorrow."

"He's your son, Cabot. No one knows him better. If you think it was best not to burden him, I'm sure you're right about that."

"So are you. He's getting attached and there's probably no way to stop that. But a reminder is a good idea. A warning would be smart."

"Maybe." She sighed. "But I'm a grown-up. I'm warned. And I don't think I'm ready to face the world yet." She met his gaze. "There was a lot of publicity when I ran out on the wedding and completely disappeared. When I resurface, that will make news, too."

"You can handle it. You're strong." He kind of wished she wasn't and would stay in his spare cabin just a while longer.

"Having the time to decompress has been great. I will have to give interviews, and I've had a lot of time to think about what I'm going to say."

"Will you tell the truth?"

"You mean that my fiancé is a lying, cheating toad?"

"Yeah, that." He grinned.

"You bet I'm going to." She looked up at him, a softness in her eyes. "But now I can talk about what happened from a position of strength, not an emotional meltdown."

"Good girl."

"The thing is," she said, "it's beginning to sink in that my feelings about wanting to stay aren't about hiding from all of that."

He knew he was going to be sorry, but he had to ask. "What, then?"

"I like Blackwater Lake and just don't want to leave."

Again he had the sensation that she was waiting for him to say something, but he couldn't go there. "We all have to do things we don't like. What will you do when you go back to your regularly scheduled life? Train for another Olympics? Continue competing? Endorsements?"

"I still have contracts. But I'm not sure about competing." She sounded disappointed, as if he hadn't said what she'd wanted him to. She looked at him. "Will you miss me?"

"That goes without saying."

"What if I *want* you to say it?"

The words and pleading in her voice were like a punch to the gut. It was a willpower test, and he would do his best to meet the challenge because if he didn't there would be hell to pay.

Ignoring the question, Cabot stood. "I think it's time to turn in. We have an early day tomorrow and should get some sleep."

"Okay. I understand." Without another word, she got up, too, and walked back to her tent, disappearing inside.

Cabot made sure the embers of the fire were completely put out. He wished there was another chore to keep him busy because he knew when he got in his sleeping bag sleep wouldn't be coming his way.

No, he would be trying to figure out a way to get the look on Kate's face out of his mind. He felt as if he'd drop-kicked a kitten. But what was he supposed to do? Acting on his feelings, even though he was pretty sure she would willingly respond, was a very bad idea.

She was leaving soon. Too soon. He would never forget how hard it was when a woman you cared about walked away. The fewer memories of Kate he had to deal with, the better.

Chapter Thirteen

Four days after returning from the campout, Kate was sitting on her bunk in the stray cabin. She'd read the same page in her book three times without comprehending what it said. With a sigh, she set it aside. Obviously even a steamy romance novel couldn't distract her from what was on her mind.

Cabot. Now, there was a hero. A living, breathing three-dimensional man with positives and even negatives that only made him more appealing.

In the wilderness she'd learned that this summer he had been hanging around the camp more than usual. Until now, that was.

She hadn't seen him at any of the activities since they'd returned.

She'd come to the conclusion that he was keeping his distance from her because she'd flat-out said she wanted him to say that he would miss her. He hadn't. The silence spoke volumes. Ty had been as cute and sweet as always, but his father was missing in action.

Looking around her small cabin, she felt a pang of regret. Oddly enough, this minimal space was more appealing than her spacious condo in California. This felt like sanctuary, a haven from her crazy, busy life. It sounded weird and overly dramatic, but this time in Blackwater Lake had repaired and replenished her soul. She loved it here.

But her time-out was coming to an end, and it would be good to repair something else. Family relationships. She'd spoken to her parents only a few times to let them know she was all right. She hadn't talked to her brother or sister at all and it was time to fix that. After pulling her cell phone from her shorts pocket and scrolling through her contacts list, she found the number she wanted and highlighted it before pressing the call button. She waited while it rang, expecting to get voice mail. A smile curved her lips when she heard her older brother's familiar voice.

"My truck better be in one piece."

She laughed at his fake growl. Obviously he'd checked his caller ID. He was a big softy with her and they both knew it. "Hi, Zach."

"You better be in one piece, too." He paused, and then she noted real concern in his voice when he asked, "Are you okay, Kate?"

"Yes. And so is Angelica." She paused for a moment, then meaningfully added, "Now."

"What did you do to her?"

"Nothing. She just stopped one day. In the rain, which was inconvenient." Although the silver lining was that she'd ended up spending the day with Cabot and the night in his bed. The sensuous memory made her shiver and brought on a yearning that was never far away.

"Kate? Are you there?"

"Yes. What?"

"Why did my truck stop? What's wrong with her? You know how much she means to me."

"Stand down, Zach. Your baby just needed a little tender loving care, and Sydney gave it to her."

"I hope he knows what he's doing." Zach's words carried a warning.

"Syd is a girl. A stunning brunette. Smart. Not at all your type."

He chuckled. "I've really missed you picking on me. I wish you'd called sooner."

"I've been in touch with Mom and Dad."

"I heard. They also said you wouldn't tell them where you are or where you've been," he pointed out.

"I needed some time."

"Say the word, Kate. I'll beat the bastard up for you." Zach clearly believed her time-out was about the aborted wedding.

She laughed at the big-brother posturing, the warm, familiar feeling it gave her. "It's so good to hear your voice."

"I mean it. If it will make you feel better, I'll mess up his pretty face."

"Ted would probably file assault and battery charges against you."

"I'd risk it."

"So not worth it to me. He's done enough damage." She'd been stupid and wouldn't be again.

Zach let loose with some colorful language before saying, "So you're not over him."

"Actually, I am. And to put a finer point

on it, I don't think there was anything to get over."

"That's a little subtle for me. You're going to have to spell it out for those of us who are touchy-feely challenged."

"I never loved him."

"How can you be so sure?"

Because everything she felt for Cabot was so much clearer, so much stronger. If she had truly loved Ted, that wouldn't be possible. "Catching Ted kissing another woman at our wedding was a blessing. Fortunately it happened before we exchanged vows. Marrying him would have been a mistake. A disaster."

"You're not just being spunky, are you?" he asked skeptically.

"Spunky? Did you seriously just call me that?"

"No."

"It sure sounded that way," she teased. "But the answer is no. I'm not putting on an act. I truly believe he did me a huge favor."

"That's a new one." Zach's tone was wry. "Cheating as a good deed."

"I'm telling the truth. Cross my heart."

"I'm glad that your heart is unscathed," he said fervently.

That wasn't completely true. Her ex hadn't

touched it, but the same couldn't be said of Cabot. The only question was how much damage he'd done.

"I'm fine. Really," she emphasized.

There was the slightest meaningful pause on the other end of the line. "That sounded as if you're trying too hard to convince me."

"Trust me, Zach. Ted is so yesterday." Cabot was today. Probably tomorrow. And as many days after that as there were until summer was over.

"So, are you ready to come home?" he asked.

"No."

"Wow. Whatever beach you're sitting on must be truly awesome."

Thinking about the nearby cabins with kids and camp counselors, Kate laughed. "You couldn't be more wrong about that."

"Okay. But wherever you are, it's obvious that you needed a break."

"Yes." She remembered that day at the church, catching her fiancé kissing one of her bridesmaids and feeling the need to run from the betrayal she'd seen with her own eyes. Maybe if she hadn't been working so hard for so long she wouldn't have run. But she simply didn't have the reserves to rationally deal with what he'd done to her. "I don't think I even realized how much I needed to get off the wheel until I got to Blackwater Lake—"

After a very long silence on the line, Zach asked, "Where are you?"

She hadn't told anyone where she was; she'd just wanted to be alone to lick her wounds without an audience. Or press. She'd only told them she was okay and would be back at the end of the summer. That was so close now that keeping her whereabouts secret didn't seem to matter anymore. In two weeks she'd be headed home because camp would be over and her verbal contract with Cabot satisfied. Emotionally not so much, but the man knew what he wanted and it didn't include her.

"I'm in Montana," she told her brother.

"Good Lord." And then he asked, "What in the world are you doing there?"

Trying not to be a romantic fool over a handsome rancher, she thought. "I'm keeping busy."

"Doing what?"

"Oh, this and that."

"Well, there's something you need to know.

It's about work. Someone has been trying to get in touch with you—"

She heard a knock on her cabin door. Although it was a little late, it was probably one of the kids. Sometimes one of them wandered over with a question. "Hold on, Zach."

She opened the door, but there was no child there. "Cabot."

"Hi," he said. Then he saw the phone and said, "Sorry. Didn't mean to interrupt."

"You didn't."

In her ear she heard a sharp tone in her brother's voice. "Who's there, Kate? Is that a man?"

"Come in," she invited Cabot. Into the phone she said, "I have to go."

"Don't hang up. I want to know what's really going on with my little sister."

"I'm fine. Stand down. I'll be back in a couple of weeks. We'll talk then."

"Kate—"

She hit the end button and met Cabot's gaze. "So, what's up?"

He nodded at her phone, which vibrated in her hand. "Someone from home?"

"Just my brother." She glanced at the caller ID and confirmed her guess. After hitting Ignore, she shut the thing off. “I’ll talk to him later.”

Zach no doubt had a lot of questions and she owed her family answers, but now wasn’t a good time. She would see them all soon enough. Right at this moment she was just so darn happy to see Cabot. It felt like forever since she’d seen him, his handsome face, the small smile that teased the corners of his mouth.

“Are you going to let the bugs in?” she asked, pointedly looking at the open doorway where he was still standing.

“I won’t be here that long.” His intense expression was completely at odds with his words.

“Okay.” Disappointment pressed against her heart. “Then why *are* you here?”

“I saw your light still on.”

She glanced over her shoulder at the book on the bed. “Yeah. I was reading.”

He shoved his fingertips into the pockets of his jeans. “Just wanted to let you know that I had a talk with Ty. About you leaving.”

“And?”

“To be honest, he got a little defensive. Said he’s not a little kid and everyone should stop treating him like one. He knows the campers and counselors are all leaving when summer's over." She saw a troubled look in his eyes when he added, "But he's going to ask if he can email you. To stay in touch."

"Of course he can. I'd love to hear from him." *And you,* she thought. With the end of her stay so near, she tried to memorize every line on his face. The shape of his nose. The strong, handsome curve of his jaw.

"Okay. Like I said, I just wanted to let you know so you wouldn't worry." But he still didn't close the door.

"Was there something else?"

This was killing her. So near, yet so far. She probably shouldn't have asked him if he was going to miss her, but she had. And all he would tell her was that it went without saying. Well, she wanted to hear him say it. Better yet, she wished he would ask her to stay.

"No. Nothing else," he said.

A jab of rejection pierced her heart, proving what she'd thought earlier—that it likely wasn't getting out of Blackwater Lake completely unscathed.

"Okay, then. You should probably get back to Ty. I know you don't like leaving him alone up at the house too long."

"He's not at the house." His voice was on the ragged side. "He's sleeping over at C.J.'s."

"Oh. Well..." He had nowhere he had to be. But he didn't want to be here. She moved to the door and started to close it. This was making her crazy, and she wished he would just go. "Anyway, it's getting late."

"Yeah. A rancher's day starts early."

"Thanks for letting me know about your talk with Ty."

He nodded but still didn't back out of the doorway. Conflict sparked in his eyes, an intense expression that revealed a battle raging inside him.

"Cabot?"

"Oh, hell—"

He stepped inside and closed the door behind him. Then he pulled her into his arms before turning to back her against the wall. At the same time he took her mouth and pressed his lower body to hers, letting her know what he wanted. His arms cushioned her back and her heart soared with the knowledge that he was protecting her. He'd lost control enough to kiss the living daylights out of her but was still taking care of her. Heat radiated through her, setting fire to her nerve endings as she kissed him back.

His mouth nibbled over her jaw and down her neck, where he touched his tongue to that spot just beneath her ear. Then he blew on the moist, sensitive place and shot tingles straight to her female core.

"I want you, Kate." The words vibrated against her skin. "I tried not to—"

"I'm glad you're here now." She shouldn't be so happy he'd failed, but she couldn't help it. "I want you, too."

His gaze searched hers for several intense moments. Both of them were breathing fast, and the harsh sound filled the tiny cabin with escalating need. Then they both moved at the same time, pulling off shirts, undoing buttons, removing pants. He'd pulled a square packet from his jeans and she recognized it as protection.

"Didn't trust your willpower?" she asked breathlessly.

"Not with you." Then he handed it to her before swinging her into his arms.

"Always be prepared?" she teased.

"Yeah, I'm a real Boy Scout. I really did want you to know I'd had a talk with Ty." Intensity simmered in his eyes. "I just wasn't sure I could say that and keep walking. If I didn't… I don't take chances."

"And you were taking me for granted?" She lifted one eyebrow teasingly, questioning.

"Not really. Never let a condom go to waste. I figured we could always wait for the sun to come up and use it to start a campfire."

"So you weren't sure about me."

"No. Yes." Need swirled in his eyes. "Am I wrong?"

"Absolutely not."

He took a couple of steps over to her bunk and gently placed her there. It was wider than a single bed, but not by a lot, so when he joined her they were skin to skin. His big hand slid over the curve of her waist and down her thigh, squeezing gently. Then he moved to her abdomen and down lower while she held her breath in anticipation.

When he touched her, she thought she would go up in flames. Reaching out a hand to the scarred pine nightstand, she found the condom and handed it over.

"Now, Cabot—" She was so breathless, the words were nearly trapped in her throat.

"I know, honey."

After putting it in place, he rolled over her and settled his weight on his forearms before slowly entering her. She wrapped her legs around his waist as he thrust into her, then matched his rhythm. He drove her higher and higher and too soon she cried out as release roared through her.

Another push, then two and he groaned, pulling her even tighter against him. They held each other for what seemed like forever as their breathing slowed and shock waves subsided.

"Oh, my—" She smiled up at him, enveloped in a warm glow.

"That goes double for me." He kissed her softly, tenderly, then levered himself off. "Hold that thought."

Completely spent, she dropped her forearm over her eyes as he walked into the tiny bathroom. Several moments later he turned off the light and returned to her bed. He lifted her enough to turn down the sheet and blanket, then slid in beside her and pulled the covers over them, curling himself around her.

The last thought she had before falling asleep in Cabot's arms was that she'd finally found the place she belonged.

The next morning Kate woke up alone in her bunk. She remembered Cabot gently easing out of the bed, trying not to wake her. She also remembered that he didn't kiss her goodbye, not even a soft touch of lips anywhere. So much for belonging.

As she showered, brushed her teeth and prepared for the day, she tried to shake the feeling of dejection, of giving up. She'd been so darn happy when he couldn't walk out the door last night without kissing her and happier than she could ever recall being when he'd made love to her. But she couldn't bury her head in the sand any longer. That wasn't love.

What they'd done in her bed was nothing more than a physical act between a man and woman. It was just sex—really fantastic sex, but without any complicated emotions—and she knew that because even casual feelings would have compelled him to kiss her goodbye. He might as well have left money on the nightstand beside the empty condom packet.

That part wasn't fair, but she wasn't in the mood to be fair this morning. She was crabby. And how could she have been so starry-eyed and spineless last night? The man had come prepared to sleep with her, for goodness' sake.

But that wasn't fair, either. She'd seen the conflict in his eyes and had felt the tension in his body. She felt a teeny, tiny bit of satisfaction that he'd given in, that she was a temptation he couldn't resist. At least last night. This morning he'd resisted her just fine.

She recalled their conversation in his bed the other time and wondered if *he* hated himself this morning.

She gave her appearance one last look in the mirror and thought at least it had been good to talk to her brother last night. By now the whole family would know she was in Blackwater Lake, Montana. That was okay because she wasn't hiding anymore.

She joined the other counselors for a busy morning of relay races, scavenger hunt and ceramics. When she walked into the kitchen for a cup of coffee just before lunch, she was hot, sweaty and covered with dried clay.

Caroline was stirring a big pot of soup and glanced up. "You look like the mud wrestler who lost. Or did someone just pull you out of quicksand?"

"Ceramics are not my best event." She sighed and looked down at the dried splotches all over her front. "Those pottery wheels can get away from you if you're not careful."

Caroline grinned. "Happens with every group. Always someone who doesn't pay attention and that stuff goes everywhere."

"And I'm a horrible warning." Kate grabbed

a mug from the cupboard and poured coffee into it. "You'd think after all these weeks I'd know when to duck."

And she didn't just mean the crafts activities.

"It happens fast," the other woman said. "You can't always see it coming."

"You'd think I'd know that, too." Absently she blew on the hot dark liquid in her cup. "I guess I'm just a slow learner. Apparently I keep making the same mistakes over and over."

Caroline put down the wooden spoon on the stainless-steel counter. She leaned back and studied Kate. "You're not just talking about ceramics now, are you?"

"What else would I be talking about?"

Kate realized this would be the perfect opening to discuss what was bothering her, but she didn't think it was professional to discuss their mutual boss, who also happened to be Caroline's good friend. Kate also knew she'd crossed the line into unprofessional territory by sleeping with him in the first place. Still, there were just a couple of weeks left. Why beat to death a situation that would soon be over?

"What I would be talking about is Cabot," the other woman said pointedly.

"I'm not sure why you would think that," Kate bluffed. "But he's not… We're not—"

"Oh, please. I'm a high school teacher and have been for a lot of years. I can tell when someone is dancing around the truth." Caroline fixed her with a teacher look that would have made the average person sing like a canary.

But Kate wasn't a teenager and didn't want to put this woman in the awkward position of taking sides. "It isn't fair or right to discuss this with you. You've known him for a long time, and it's not appropriate for you to be caught in the middle."

"Why don't you let me worry about all that?" Caroline said gently. "He's my friend, yes, but so are you. I've grown fond of you. It's obvious to me something happened that's bothering you. And if the choices are ceramics or Cabot, my money is on him. What did he do?"

If Kate said he hadn't kissed her goodbye when he'd left her cabin that morning, it would open up a whole messy can of worms. *Keep it simple.* "Well, I guess you could say I'm attracted to him."

"Tell me something I don't know." Caroline's tone was teasing. "In fact, everyone knows. One look and it's pretty clear that the two of you have the hots for each other."

Really? Everyone? Diane had noticed differences in Cabot and clearly suspected it had something to do with Kate. Yes, she quivered like crazy when she was around him. If that qualified as "the hots," she was guilty as charged. But she wanted more, something deep and lasting. This conversation was pointless.

Kate took a sip of coffee. "Oh, well, I don't know about that—"

"I'm really going to stick my nose in where it doesn't belong," Caroline interrupted. "But I think you've slept with him."

Kate wanted so badly to say he'd started it, but she wasn't twelve. And she'd enthusiastically participated.

Cheeks hot with something that was a mixture of guilt and shame, she met the other woman's gaze. "I have."

"I didn't really know for sure. Just took a shot." Caroline smiled, a pleased expression on her attractive features. "I'm so glad."

Now she was confused. "You are?"

"Absolutely. What?" the other woman questioned. "You thought I'd be upset?"

"Maybe." Kate shrugged. "At the very least I thought you'd be protective of him."

"Oh, I am. When the situation calls for it. But this isn't one of those times." Caroline's expression was soft and maternal. "You're good for him, Kate."

"I am?" She blinked, then gripped her coffee mug so tightly her knuckles turned white. "Could have fooled me."

"He's very closed off since his wife left. She really did a number on him."

"She still is doing a number on him," Kate corrected.

"You know she passed away?"

"I do." No way would Kate share about being with him when he got the call because of having spent the night in his bed. "And he wanted me to stand by when he broke the news to Ty."

"You're good for that boy, too," Caroline observed. "So explain to me how that woman is still messing with him."

"He's in love with her and always will be."

"Did he tell you that?" Caroline's blue eyes narrowed skeptically.

"Almost. He told me his father never

stopped loving his mother even though she left. He was a one-woman man and Cabot takes after him."

"In a lot of ways he does," Caroline agreed. "They both have a connection to the land and family. But not in relationships. That woman walked out and left him with a newborn. It took him a while to get through all the steps of grief over it, but I'd bet everything I've got that he stopped loving her a long time ago."

"I'm not so sure."

"He's different with you," Caroline persisted. "He's lighter somehow—his spirit, I mean. He hired me to run the camp when Ty was a baby and he had his hands full with everything. But this is the first summer I've seen him so involved. And Diane told me how he acted on the campout. The only difference around here is you."

"I'm having a hard time believing that," Kate confessed. "He's really resistant."

"He's built up some pretty high, thick walls, but if you give it time, I think they can be penetrated."

"If it's not in the next couple weeks, I won't be around to see that."

"Why not? You could stick here if you wanted to. After all, if your life was firing on all cylinders, you wouldn't be here in the first place."

Kate couldn't dispute that. And she wasn't looking forward to leaving, which was pretty telling. She loved Blackwater Lake, and that had nothing to do with Cabot and how she felt about him.

"You have a point about that. But two wrongs don't make a right."

"And giving up without a fight is the coward's way out. What if he's your soul mate?"

"What if *she* was *his?*" Kate shot back.

"Sometimes you have to take a leap of faith to get what you want."

"A little encouragement from him would make it a lot less scary."

"No pain, no gain."

Kate knew the other woman was sincere and began to wonder if she might be right. Caroline certainly had known him a long time. What if Kate was giving up too soon?

"I'll give it some thought," she agreed. "And thanks for talking with me. I really do feel a lot better."

"Good." Caroline smiled. "I love playing Cupid. It's so rewarding when—"

A strange sound interrupted her, something completely out of place. Usually the quiet here by the lake and mountains was absolute, but Kate swore the noise was the *whap whap* of helicopter rotors and it was moving closer and getting a lot louder. She and Caroline looked at each other and without a word walked to the door, then went outside onto the porch.

Sure enough, they weren't the only ones who'd heard. All the kids and counselors were gathered outside, watching as a helicopter set down in the open area by Cabot's house. On the side of the chopper were the letters *ESPN*.

Kate made an educated guess that this had something to do with her and took off at a run up the slight rise. She stopped beside Cabot, and both of them watched as a man in an expensive suit and tie stepped out of the chopper. He approached with hand outstretched to Cabot and the two shook.

"I'm John Crowley, vice president in charge of televised sports for ESPN." He looked at her. "You're not an easy woman to locate, Miss Scott. But I've got a proposition for you, and I think you're going to like it."

Chapter Fourteen

"Dad, is Kate going to fly away on that helicopter?"

Cabot saw the anxiety in his son's eyes. The boy had come running with everyone else from the camp when the guy in charge of sports for ESPN had arrived. He'd asked to speak with Kate privately, and Cabot had offered his house. They were still talking, as far as he knew. He was in the barn with his son, fielding questions that he had no answers for.

"I don't know, Ty," he said. "I could sure use your help mucking out this stall."

The boy only nodded, but the wheels were turning. Cabot had no illusions that the interrogation was over. This was just the eye of the hurricane, and he was bracing for the storm to come.

He and Ty assembled shovels, a wheelbarrow and a pitchfork to remove the dirty hay and replace it. The work was messy and sweaty, but sometimes a guy needed something like this. Now was one of those times.

Ty shoveled up some muck. "That man must be pretty rich if he could come here in a helicopter."

That thought had also occurred to Cabot. "Yeah."

"Why do you think he wants to talk to her?"

"He said he's in charge of sports broadcasting, so it probably has something to do with that."

Cabot had quickly realized that Kate was an even bigger deal than he knew. One picture was worth a thousand words, and the helicopter was quite a visual pointing to the fact that she was way out of his league.

He dumped a shovelful of dirty hay into the wheelbarrow. "Remember I told you she won Olympic medals in skeet shooting?"

"Yeah. That's her best event."

"Well, when someone is an expert and a

competition is on TV, they like to get that person to explain things to the people watching."

"Oh." The boy leaned on his shovel, obviously thinking that over. "If she does that, will she have to go? I mean before summer's over?"

"It's probably best not to speculate about that. We don't even know for sure that's what it's about." But he was pretty sure they wouldn't send a suit in a helicopter to discuss the summer-camp program.

This was a big deal.

"I don't want her to go, Dad."

"I know, son."

It was official. The talk he'd had with Ty had not prepared the kid for her leaving. Cabot knew better than his son that there was no way to prepare yourself for the void of losing someone you cared about. Tyler cared about Kate and he wasn't the only one in this family who did.

He'd known that when he stuck that condom in his pocket last night in case he couldn't make himself walk away after telling her about his talk with Ty. But as soon as he'd pocketed the thing, there was no way he could keep himself from having her. He realized that now. On some level he'd already made up his mind to take her to bed.

Some indefinable thing about Kate Scott drew him like a moth to a flame. And it wasn't just sex, although that was fantastic. He just really liked her, everything about her. Especially the way she'd taken Tyler under her wing.

"Dad, I have an idea."

"Oh?" Cabot knew he wasn't going to like this. "What is it, son?"

"You should talk to her. Tell her you want her to stay."

"I didn't say that." He saw the boy working up to a protest and jumped in before the words came out. "You said you don't want her to go and I said I understand how you feel. That's all."

"It's the same thing."

"No, it's not." Cabot couldn't let himself want her to stay. He couldn't cross that line; he couldn't take the chance. If it went badly, and he had every reason to believe it would, he might never make it back. "But that doesn't mean you can't tell her how you feel."

He heard muffled footsteps on the hard-packed dirt path that ran down the center of the barn. Seconds later Kate appeared.

"Here you are," she said to Cabot, then smiled at Ty. "I've been looking everywhere for you."

"Hi, Kate. What did that guy want?" The boy was clearly happy to see her.

Cabot wanted to think he wasn't, but it would be a lie. He couldn't look at her hard enough or long enough.

"The helicopter was pretty cool, no?" An undeniable undercurrent of excitement hummed through her. "I talked to my brother, Zach, last night. Apparently he told them where to find me. It was about a job offer."

"They didn't waste any time." They must've wanted her bad. Cabot knew exactly how that felt. "What's the proposal?"

"A national championship is coming up in a couple of weeks, and they want me to provide color, context and commentary on my sport."

"I see."

"He said they saw the magazine cover and liked my look. They think that people will be interested in my story, and that will boost the ratings for skeet the way Danica Patrick has done for NASCAR. The objective is to get airtime experience before the summer Olympics, which aren't that far away."

"You sound excited." That was the exact opposite of how he felt.

"I'm flattered, for sure. And it's always nice to be asked." She glanced down at the front of her legs, the dried dirt on her shirt and shorts. "And they still wanted me, even though I look as if I've been dipped in quicksand."

He thought she'd never looked more beautiful than she did at this moment. But he couldn't afford to give in to that feeling. "So you accepted."

"That's what I'd like to talk to you about." She grew serious and looked at Tyler, who was listening to every word and soaking it up like a sponge. "Kiddo, could I talk to your dad alone for a few minutes?"

"You're going to leave, aren't you?" His voice had threads of anger and hurt mixing together.

"There's a whole lot to consider, sweetie."

"Ty, we talked about this. You knew Kate was only staying until the end of summer."

"But she likes it here," he cried. "I know she does."

"You're right about that, Ty. I do love Blackwater Lake and the ranch. But—"

"She has a career," Cabot interjected. "And

this is a really good opportunity for her. Do you understand?"

"Yes." But the expression in his eyes said different.

"Just let me talk to your dad for a little bit," she pleaded. "Then I'll come find you and let you know what's happening."

"You won't leave without saying goodbye?"

"Of course not. I promise," she said. "If I go."

"Okay." The tone said he would do as requested but wasn't happy about it. He dragged the shovel behind him as he walked out of the stall and toward the barn door, leaving them alone.

Cabot set his own shovel against the stall fence, then turned back, carefully and deliberately standing a few feet away from her. "So, what did you tell them?"

"I turned it down."

That shocked him. "Why? Isn't it a really good opportunity?"

"It's what I've been working for."

"And you told them no?"

"I did."

He shook his head. "But you're ready to go back. All set to rat out the cheating scumbag about what he did. Face the world."

"But I don't want that world anymore." Her eyes pleaded with him to understand. "Staying here on the ranch, here in Blackwater Lake, is what will make me happy."

Call him cynical, but his wife had said she wanted to stay, too, and that hadn't worked out so well. "What would you have said to this offer if you'd never come here?"

"But I did."

"Humor me. Think about this. What if you hadn't driven into Blackwater Lake in your wedding gown and stayed for the summer camp? What would you have said to a sportscasting gig that you've worked really hard for?"

She thought about it for a moment as emotions swirled in her eyes. "I would have said yes. But I did come here and stay for the summer—"

He held up a hand to stop her. "That's what I thought."

"Cabot, listen to me. Being here with you and Ty has changed my perspective and priorities. What we have is special and I'm not willing to give that up."

"It's a summer fling."

"You don't mean that. Not after last night."

He met her gaze and forced himself not to

look away so that she would see this was for the best. He also fought the overwhelming urge to pull her into his arms and beg her not to go. But if he did that and she stayed, missing out on all the opportunities waiting for her, eventually she'd resent him. He would lose her either way, so why prolong the inevitable?

"Yeah, I do mean it. We both know this isn't going anywhere. You have a once-in-a-lifetime opportunity and should take it. You should go."

"You're only saying that because circumstances made ranch life your career choice. Maybe you feel deprived of having the option or this is about the fact that your wife wasn't satisfied with her decision. But for some people, the life you live every single day is a dream."

"Dreams are nothing but a romantic notion before reality hits you where it hurts."

Kate stared at him for several moments, surprise and hurt filling her eyes. Then a single fat tear rolled down her cheek, and he nearly lost his resolve.

"Don't, Kate," he pleaded. "You'll see. This is the best thing for both of us. A clean break."

"There's nothing clean about this." Anger chased the wounded expression from her face. "You think you're being noble, preserving that nice-guy image by helping people who are down on their luck. And when you didn't know about me, everything was fine. I fit into the mold of acceptable, someone who got through the barrier."

"Look, this is—"

She held up her hand. "You had your say—now it's my turn. All was well until you found out I could actually take care of myself, but you started putting up different walls. Taking me to bed was okay as long as it was just temporary. But you're so worried about taking another chance that I think you're glad about this offer. It takes the heat off."

Her words hit very close to the mark, and he didn't like that at all. "Is psychobabble part of your Olympic regimen? If so, you need more training. You're way off target."

"Is that so?" She glared at him. "Well, even Olympic gold medalists miss what they aim at from time to time."

Without another word, she turned and walked out of the barn, head held high.

Cabot stared at the space where she'd been standing just a moment ago. He had that feeling of making a spontaneous purchase, then having buyer's remorse. Before he could puzzle that out, he heard a noise.

"Is someone there?"

"It's me, Dad." Tyler walked into the stall.

"I thought you went back to hang out with the other kids."

The boy shook his head. "You're probably gonna be mad and I'm sorry, but I had to."

"What did you do?"

"I listened to you and Kate talking."

Cabot read disappointment and censure in the eight-year-old's eyes. He saw a maturity far beyond his years, something Cabot had had in his own gaze as a kid.

"You know it's wrong to eavesdrop," he scolded.

"I had to," Ty said again. "No one tells a kid what's going on and I really needed to know."

"So you're aware that Kate is leaving."

"You told her to go," Ty accused. "She wasn't going to take that job. She told the helicopter guy no. She wanted to stay here because she cares about us."

"It's complicated." He winced as the words came out of his mouth. He'd proved what his son had just said about adults talking down to him.

"Yeah. That's what grown-ups always tell kids. And maybe I don't understand everything, but I get this. You really blew it, Dad. Girls sure aren't *your* best event." Then he turned and walked out, too.

Cabot lifted his Stetson and dragged his fingers through his hair before replacing his hat. He looked at the dirty hay around him and thought it was ironic that the whole crappy scene had happened here.

Ty was right. Love wasn't his best event, but heading off trouble was, and that was just what he'd done. Although the sinking feeling in his gut was starting to feel like a different kind of trouble.

The day after Kate left the ranch, Cabot was getting the cold shoulder from his son and dirty looks from everyone else. Or maybe he was imagining that because he felt lower than a snake's belly. Ty did say that Kate had kept her promise and said goodbye to him. He also shared that she'd told the boy she was taking the job and if he wanted to know why she couldn't come back here when it was over he should ask his dad.

But Ty hadn't asked him anything, apparently assuming that Cabot was completely hopeless with girls. That was what he'd been trying to tell everyone, so why was it such a big surprise when it all imploded?

For the first time in his life, the wide-open spaces were closing in on him, so Cabot had decided to go into Blackwater Lake for lunch. Ty declined the invitation to come along, opting to hang out with the camp kids, so Cabot walked into the Grizzly Bear Diner alone. It was half past noon and the booths were mostly full. People here and there occupied the swivel stools at the counter.

He took his usual seat, the one where he'd been sitting when Kate had shown up in her wrinkled wedding dress. Michelle Crawford was there, just as she'd been that day to interview the beautiful stranger who'd ended up making such a ding in his life.

The diner owner gave him a big smile. "Cabot, it's good to see you."

"You, too, Michelle." Even more, it was nice to see a friendly face. "How's the family?"

"Good. Emma and Justin are planning their wedding."

"I hope to get an invitation."

"The whole town will get one," she promised. "We have so much to celebrate."

A year ago Michelle, her husband and their three sons had been reunited with the daughter/sister who'd been kidnapped and taken from them as a baby. She'd come looking for her family and found the love of her life in Dr. Justin Flint, who worked at the medical clinic in town. It was nice to see good things happen to good people. Cabot considered himself an upstanding guy, but he held out no expectation of rainbows and roses. It just wasn't in the cards for him.

"Coffee?" Michelle asked.

He nodded. "And a burger."

"Coming right up." She wrote out the order and handed it to the cook working the grill behind her, then grabbed the coffeepot and a mug. "So what's up with Kate?"

"Why do you ask?"

"Seriously?" Pouring his coffee, she glanced up quickly and met his gaze. Her own was wry. "You did see the helicopter, right?"

"Yeah. I was there." He'd have been better off rounding up strays in an isolated canyon far away from what had happened yesterday. Especially the part where he'd talked to Kate in the barn. "How did you know about that?"

"Caroline called me." She rested the pot on the counter. "We knew Kate was a big deal when her picture was on that magazine cover. But who sends a helicopter? That really makes a statement."

"Yup." He lifted his mug and blew on the hot coffee.

"I'm dying to hear about it. So, where is she?" Michelle persisted.

Cabot figured there was no point in beating around the bush. If he did, the woman would just call Caroline and jump-start Blackwater Lake's very efficient information network. "She's gone."

"What?" The woman looked genuinely surprised.

"She left."

"For a job." Michelle studied him intently. "She'll be back, right?"

Cabot shook his head. "For good."

"Why would she do that? She loves this town."

"How do you know?" he asked.

"You could just tell. And she said so more than once." She frowned. "Everyone liked her. She's not a stuck-up city girl who couldn't stand being in a town where the closest mall is an hour away."

Like his wife, he thought. "I didn't realize you knew her that well."

"Actually, I don't because you kept her pretty busy at camp. But I heard. Sydney McKnight got to know her, though."

A woman had just walked in the door and sat down on the swivel stool beside him. "Did I hear my name? Are you talking about me, Michelle?"

"I never miss a chance to talk about anyone, and everyone comes in this diner sooner or later. It's gossip central. You should know that, Sydney."

"Right." Sydney looked at him. "Hi, Cabot. I haven't seen you since the day Kate's truck broke down. How are you?"

He'd been better but was glad she'd interrupted the conversation. Kate was the last person he wanted to talk about today. "I'm great. How's business at the garage?"

"Good. We're really busy." The pretty brunette glanced from him to Michelle. "So, I'm dying to hear about the helicopter at your ranch yesterday."

And here we go again, he thought. He looked at the two women, then sipped his coffee without answering.

Michelle had no problem filling the silence.

"He was just telling me that Kate is gone and she's not coming back."

"She is?" Syd sounded surprised. "I don't believe that."

"Believe it." Cabot remembered the anger and hurt on Kate's face, the tear that had rolled down her cheek. He would never forget how she'd looked and his part in it. What he'd done was for the best, he repeated to himself. She would realize that soon enough.

"I don't understand," Syd said. "I saw her not that long ago, and it sounded like she would be here for the long term."

"You probably misunderstood." If there was a God in heaven, his hamburger would come any second now. Although when women were determined to get information, a man wanting to eat probably wasn't going to stop them from asking questions.

"I'm sure I got what she was saying. She was very clear that Blackwater Lake felt like home to her." The young woman looked puzzled. "That leaves only one possibility."

"That's what I'm thinking," Michelle chimed in.

"Do I want to know?" he asked, already knowing the answer.

"Probably not," Syd said. "What happened with you two?"

"I'd like to know, too." The diner owner stared at him.

The real answer was that it was his fault Kate wasn't here. He couldn't be the right man, couldn't tell her what she wanted to hear. But that was better kept to himself.

"The simple truth is that ESPN sent somebody important to offer her a job. She took it." He cradled the coffee mug between his palms and looked at each woman in turn. "End of story."

"I don't think so." Syd's dark eyes narrowed suspiciously. "What did you do to her?"

"Nothing."

Well, he'd slept with her, but he didn't think that counted. These two were digging for relationship stuff and there wasn't one between him and Kate. He'd been careful to make sure she knew that up front. Technically he hadn't done anything but stick to the established rules.

"Not buying it." Michelle shook her head as if he was dumb as a post. "She fit in here. I, for one, would never have predicted that she would, what with her being a runaway bride and all."

"I wish I'd seen her that day," Syd commented wistfully.

That was a sight Cabot would never forget. Along with her and Ty laughing together. The sight of Kate standing by the lake with moonlight shining in her hair. Memories of waking up beside her in his bed. The disappointment in her eyes when he'd trashed her romantic notions.

"I guess she changed her mind," he said.

"Michelle is right. She fit seamlessly into Blackwater Lake, and not everyone does. People really liked her. She never played the cover-girl card, never acted like a diva. Always down-to-earth. I'd have bet money on her sticking around. Unless…" Sydney gave him a pointed look.

Cabot gave it right back. "What?"

"You're the variable." She toyed with the straw in the diet soda Michelle had set in front of her. "Something happened between you and Kate. What did you do to her?"

Nothing that he wanted to talk about, but he wasn't going to get to wiggle off this hook that easily. Walking out was an option, but he was no coward. He might as well give them the facts so that when the story spread, and it would, at least the truth would be out there.

"The fact is, she got a job offer. ESPN wants her to do commentary on a nationally televised competition. It's sort of an audition for the summer Olympics in a couple of years. I gave her my blessing."

He'd told her to go. If he'd understood the emptiness of her leaving, he wasn't so sure he would have sent her away.

"I get it now," Michelle said, shaking her head again.

"Me, too." Sydney sighed, and the way she looked at him now was similar to how the summer-camp staff did.

The only way to describe it was *pity.* And the only satisfaction he got was that they stopped grilling him like raw meat. That was small comfort when he felt as if he was losing everything. When had this community, the one he'd always loved and counted on, started working against him?

The answer was simple. It had happened the day a woman with light brown, sun-streaked hair walked into the Grizzly Bear Diner wearing a strapless wedding dress and four-inch satin heels.

As badly as he wanted to put her down as being a runner, that wasn't the case. After all, he'd given her his blessing to go.

Chapter Fifteen

Cabot left his house and headed down the rise to the camp compound. He was glad that only a few days were left until the last group of kids would be gone. Then he'd help Caroline and the counselors close everything down until next year. Equipment, linens and mattresses had to be inventoried and stored for the winter. Also, he always readied the stray cabin in case someone needed it.

And that made him think of Kate. Of course, it didn't take all that much for his thoughts to go there.

Just thinking her name sent a stab of pain and loneliness shooting through him. She'd been gone more than a week, and the feelings of missing her just kept getting worse. Those flowery sayings about time healing all wounds was pure crap, in his opinion. Time wasn't helping at all.

People in town thought he had a screw loose for letting her go. They were entitled to their view, but not one had a wife who'd walked out because she hated her life on his ranch. Ty was speaking to him again, but clearly he missed Kate and talked about her a lot, which was its own kind of hell.

Until that day when the helicopter had touched down and the kid had eavesdropped in the barn, Ty hadn't even been aware of what was going on between Cabot and Kate. The irony was that he and his son were drawn to the same woman, but that was no comfort.

He walked into the dining room, empty now until dinner in a couple of hours. There were no warm bodies or noise in here, but it was still full of memories. Eating dinner with Kate on the patio. Watching the kids soak up every word about surviving in the wilderness. Cooking bugs. That made him smile, and it was about the only thing that could have.

"Something amusing?"

Cabot looked over at Caroline. He'd been

so wrapped up in thinking about Kate that he hadn't heard the woman approach. "No. Nothing's funny."

"We're a little short-tempered this morning, aren't we?" Her eyebrows lifted questioningly. "Did someone get up on the wrong side of the bed?"

If he'd known how empty his bed would feel without Kate in it, he would never have taken her there. Those memories were some of the most tormenting. And it wouldn't do any good to bunk in the stray cabin to escape them because he'd held her in his arms there, too.

"I'm fine." But even he heard the edge in his voice.

"Yeah. I can tell."

"Everyone's got an opinion, but no one is walking in my boots. Don't start with me, Caroline."

"Start what?" she asked innocently.

"Kate," he all but growled. "I don't want to talk about her."

"Okay. So what are you doing here?"

"Just wondered if you have enough help for shutting the operation down after these kids leave."

"We could probably use one extra pair of

hands," she acknowledged. "Seeing as we're suddenly a body short."

Accusation was in her tone, but he managed to ignore that. "Okay. I'll bring one of the hired hands with me to help when the time comes." He glanced out the sliding glass door leading to the patio. The kids were wearing bathing suits and drifting back from the lake with towels draped around their necks. "How about now? Are things okay, with one body short, I mean?"

"As good as can be expected."

He knew how that felt because he missed that spectacular body, along with her sassy sense of humor and quick wit. But he wondered what Caroline meant. "What's going on?"

"I'm bummed that the kids who came here for a ranch experience will get their money's worth, but it won't be as rich an experience as it might have been. If Kate was still here to teach survival skills, I mean."

"They'll get enough. It always was before she ever showed up." In her damn wedding dress looking like a fashion-show refugee.

"What about Ty?" Caroline leaned a hip against one of the long picniclike tables.

"I don't know what you're getting at." He'd

come here to talk about camp shutdown, but this was wandering off the trail into personal territory. He was lost and no amount of survival skills would help him find his way out. "Frankly, I don't think I want to know where you're going with this."

"Ask me if I care." She was obstinate, no question about it, but the pigheaded look on her face was new. "Your son is hurting, Cabot, and you know it."

"He'll get over it."

"Yeah. Life has a way of moving on, but it will change him. As you well know."

"He barely knew Kate." In fact, his son had known her longer than his own mother. "And I'm not sure what you want me to do about it. She left for a job."

Caroline ignored that. "Kate wasn't here a long time—I'll grant you that. But Ty got a glimpse of what it would be like to have a mom. She was good to him and good for him."

Cabot shifted his feet, feeling not only his own hurt and betrayal, but also his son's. "I can't force someone to stay. People move in and out of his life and I have no power to control who he does or doesn't become attached to."

"In most cases that's true. But it's different with Kate."

"No, it's not." He already knew she was unique, but he would argue the point all day long. "She was always only temporary and Ty knew that. I talked to him about it." Because Kate had insisted so that his son wouldn't get hurt. Fat lot of good the conversation had done.

"She didn't act temporary." Caroline shook her head sadly. "And she didn't feel that way. It's just not the same without her here."

Cabot knew exactly what she meant, but no way would he say anything to agree with her. It was better to let her believe he'd gotten up on the wrong side of the bed than confirm how miserable he was. And she would know. He couldn't put anything over on this woman.

"She's not irreplaceable," he said defensively.

"You're so wrong about that." The stubborn look shifted into her eyes again, and around the edges he saw pity. "And if you don't go after her, you're a damn fool."

"No. It would be foolish to chase after her just to get smacked down a second time."

"That's your father talking, Cabot," she said gently.

"What are you saying?" As soon as the words were out of his mouth he knew it was a mistake. Walking out rather than listening to this would have been a better option. The only reason he didn't was out of respect for this woman.

"When your mom left, you were just a vulnerable kid and your dad was shocked and hurt. Everything he was feeling got passed down to you. All the betrayal and bitterness. The wariness and lack of trust, even though he never stopped loving her."

"It wasn't his fault."

"I know," she said softly. "But the damage was done and he couldn't help it. It's just bad damn luck that your mom didn't love him enough to stay and he couldn't love anyone else and move on. He was a one-woman man."

"Yeah."

"And to make matters worse, you finally took a chance and, as luck would have it, picked someone cut from the same cloth as your mother."

"Dixon curse," he said angrily.

"Maybe. Or it could just be you were young and stupid. Ready to settle down and decided to settle for her and called it love."

Her words had a ring of truth. “And your point? I know you’ve got one.”

“I’m willing to bet that you weren’t really in love with Jennifer.” She met his gaze, and her eyes clearly said *pay attention.* “Sometimes you don’t get it until you fall hard and fast for real.”

“There might be something to that,” he conceded.

“The problem is, Kate thinks you were in love with your ex and still are. Pining for her like your dad did for your mom.”

“How do you know?”

“She told me.” Caroline shrugged. “We were in the kitchen together a lot. Women talk and she came right out and said it.”

Cabot knew Kate thought that and he hadn’t tried very hard to set her straight. On some level he’d assumed if she was under that impression, they could avoid a mess like he was in now. He no longer qualified for the young-and-stupid defense. He was older but definitely still not wiser where women were concerned.

“It doesn’t matter, Caroline. She still left.”

“Because you told her to go.”

“It was the right thing to do.” Although he wasn’t so sure he believed that anymore.

"Maybe. To a point. The truth is she has a career and obligations, but that doesn't mean compromises can't be made. Things worked out. It makes a person glad that you don't work for this country's diplomatic corps." She gave him a wry look. "Kate did what you told her to because of what she believes, that there's no hope of having a life with you."

"She walked out. Nothing can be done now."

"Oh, please, Cabot Dixon. If you really believe that, you're as dense as they come."

"I hope you don't say that to your high school students."

"It gets some sugarcoating and a gentler touch," she admitted. "But the same message."

"Which is?"

"If you don't go after her, you're not nearly as smart as I know you are." She straightened away from the table and put a hand on his arm. "The two of you love each other."

"How can you be so sure?" Cabot knew what she said was the truth but wondered what had given him away.

"Just the way you look at each other. It's right there on your faces. And what a shame it would be to miss out on all that could be yours just because you're too stubborn, stupid and scared to go after her and admit you made a mistake when you sent her away."

Suddenly it hit him. Caroline was right. About everything. "I don't even know where to find her."

"I do. When she said goodbye, she gave me her contact information, including her mother's phone number. She said from now on they would always know where she is. I've talked to the woman. She's very nice, by the way." Caroline grinned. "What can I say? I'm a people person. It's a gift. You can thank me later."

"Caroline, I could kiss you."

"I'll take it." She lifted her cheek, then gave him a teacher look. "I just hope you haven't messed this up so badly it can't be fixed."

He planted one on her at the same time he prayed that Kate would hear him out.

A couple of weeks after leaving Blackwater Lake, Kate was in Nevada for the Western Regional Championships at the Clark County Shooting Complex. This would be her first on-camera experience and she was nervous. The sports network had given her a crash course in the basics of broadcasting, and a commentator would be running the show. He would ask questions and prompt her to provide context and color to the program. She liked him; he'd told her to just talk about the sport she knew and loved.

She could do that; it was the adding-color part that concerned her. Since she'd left Cabot's ranch, it felt as if all the color had seeped out of her life. She ate, drank, talked, laughed, worked. She went through the motions of living, but it was all in black and white. *Miserable* didn't begin to describe how she felt, but she still had a job to do.

Right now she was sitting in the mobile hair-and-makeup trailer, which was a big tricked-out motor home with beauty stations set up. Except for Andrea, who was getting her camera ready, she was alone. Through the window in front of her she could see the cloudless blue sky and mountains that looked as if they'd been carved from rock. Pretty in their own way, but not a single evergreen tree in sight. It wasn't Montana.

She missed Blackwater Lake desperately, and the thought brought tears to her eyes. Crying couldn't happen. It would ruin her makeup, and Andrea would have to fix the damage. Some professional she was.

The young blue-eyed blonde was applying her mascara. She frowned. "Do you have allergies? Nevada is different from California, and something could be making your eyes water."

Something was, but it had nothing to do with flora, fauna or the fact that it was dry as a bone in the desert. She simply missed Cabot, and her heart hurt every time she thought about not being able to see him.

"I'm so sorry, Andrea."

The other woman waved a hand. "No big deal. It's nothing that can't be touched up."

"I don't mean to be so much trouble."

"Are you kidding?" The young woman took a small makeup sponge and blotted under Kate's eyes. "I've worked with trouble, and you don't even rate in the top ten."

"Still, I don't want to give you more work to do."

"It isn't allergies, is it?"

Not unless she was allergic to loving and losing.

Andrea took another sponge and ran it through a small container of light tan–colored concealer. "I heard rumors. About you and some rancher in Montana."

"How could anyone know about that?"

Kate had told her family what had happened, and Zach had wanted to beat up the rancher in question. The thought made her tear up again.

The other woman noticed. “I’m sorry. I have no idea how this stuff gets started.”

“Rumors and gossip remind me of Blackwater Lake.”

“Where’s that?”

“Montana.”

“Where the rancher is?”

Kate nodded. “It’s a small town and news travels fast. The people who live there take great pride in that.”

“How did you find this place?” Andrea shrugged. “We might as well talk about this. Get it out of your system and maybe you’ll stop crying.”

She didn’t think that would happen, but it was worth a try. “You know that I ran out on my wedding?”

“Yeah. When you dropped off the radar it was a big story. For what it’s worth, you did the right thing, walking out on the cheating jerk.”

“Sure dodged a bullet there.”

When she’d returned from Montana, one of the first things she did was a series of interviews to set the record straight. Some of the fallout was that her ex lost a fair number of high-profile sports figures he represented, including Kate. It hadn't taken her long to find excellent representation, a guy who made sure she took advantage of this opportunity for some terrific publicity that highlighted her new gig as a sports commentator. Now it occurred to her that the press might have been digging into her Blackwater Lake experience, which was how the romantic rumors had started.

She continued her story. "After I caught him kissing another woman, I grabbed the first set of car keys I saw and they happened to belong to my brother's old truck. I got in, still wearing my wedding gown, and drove until I was too tired to drive anymore. That happened to be Blackwater Lake."

In spite of how badly things had turned out with Cabot, she would never regret finding the town, the beauty and majesty of the lake and mountains. Knowing the people. She was keeping in touch with Caroline and Sydney.

"Is the rumor about the rancher true?" Andrea asked.

Kate nodded. "Cabot Dixon. He's smart, funny, a little brooding, which is sexy. Wonderful father to an eight-year-old boy. Tyler."

She missed him, too.

"What happened?" The other woman was teasing and tweaking her hair.

"I worked at his summer camp. He felt sorry for the runaway bride and took me in."

"No. I mean personally—between the two of you."

Kate had fallen in love with him—that was what had happened. And he'd broken her heart. "I was supposed to stay until the end of summer, but the network sent a helicopter to find me."

"I heard about that." Andrea frowned. "Cabot didn't try to stop you from leaving?"

"He urged me to take the job." *Because he didn't want me.* It was as simple as that. Her eyes filled with tears again. "I don't think the talking-about-this therapy is working very well. Probably we should change the subject."

"Too soon?" When she nodded, Andrea said, "Okay. Then let's talk about your brother."

"What's there to say? Like all brothers, he's annoying and endearing in equal parts."

"Don't forget cute." Andrea had a dreamy look in her eyes. Apparently Zach's visit to the sports newsroom had made an impression. "Is he single?"

"Yes, but you don't want—" A knock on the door interrupted.

"Probably they want you in the booth. Come in," she called out.

The door opened and a man wearing a formal black tuxedo walked in. Kate saw him in the mirror and her heart started hammering in her chest. "Cabot—"

Andrea gasped and gawked. "The rancher?"

He held out his hand. "Cabot Dixon. Nice to meet you."

"Andrea Tillson. Where's the cowboy hat?" She looked him up and down. "You look like you just filmed a champagne commercial or ran out on a wedding."

"There's a good reason for that."

He looked awkward and uncomfortable but so incredibly handsome that Kate could hardly stand it. "Where's Tyler?"

"With C.J.'s family."

"How did you find me?"

"Caroline shared your contact information with me. I talked with your brother and he told me where to go."

That was when she noticed the bruise near his eye. "He made you work for the information, didn't he?"

Cabot brushed a knuckle over his cheek. "He's everything a big brother should be."

Kate didn't know whether to laugh or cry. "Why did you come?"

He looked at Andrea. "Would it be all right if I talked to her alone?"

"Sure. Of course." She looked at her watch. "You've got about a half hour before your call."

The girl walked out, and Kate was alone with him. She took off the plastic cape protecting her silk shirt and denim jacket from the heavy makeup and stood to face him. If there was a God in heaven she would be able to keep him from seeing that she'd been crying over him just minutes ago.

"It seems as if you've gone to a lot of trouble to find me and I really can't figure out why." She tried to be cool as she stared at the face she'd missed so much. The one she'd never expected to see again. He had a point to make; the tuxedo was a big clue. "We said everything necessary that last day on the ranch."

"No, we didn't." He ran his index finger around the starched collar of the formal white shirt. "I have more I want to tell you."

She looked at her wristwatch. "Okay. You've got twenty-eight minutes."

"Then I'll get right to the point. I'm not in love with my ex-wife. That was over long before she died. If I grieved at all, it was for Ty and the fact that he might miss her being part of his life."

He looked sincere and she believed him. "Okay. If that's all—"

"It's not." He took a step closer and looked down. "I found out that I am a one-woman man just like my dad was. But my wife wasn't that woman."

"Who is?" Her head was spinning at the pace of the revelations.

His brown eyes darkened with intensity. "You are."

"I am? You sure have a funny way of showing it."

He moved his shoulders uncomfortably. "I feel stupid in this tux but not as stupid as when I told you to go." He reached out and took her hand, linked his fingers with hers. "I was telling the truth about not wanting to stand in your way. I never want you to have regrets or give up anything for me."

"Oh, Cabot—"

"The thing is, I completely blew that. Shut

the door because of my hang-ups. I've since been educated about the fact that couples make things work by reaching compromises. I want you to follow your dreams—as long as you always come home to me."

"Are you sure?" Her heart nearly stopped. After all the unhappiness, it was hard to take in what he was saying. "I understand why this is hard for you—"

He touched a finger to her lips. "Very sure, and I'll tell you why."

"I'm listening."

"I take after my dad and it's not in my DNA to stop loving you. And I *do* love you, Kate. I think I have from the first moment I saw you in that wedding dress at the Grizzly Bear Diner. So, I really hope you can forgive me for being so stubborn and stupid."

If anyone needed forgiveness it was her, for enjoying his groveling just a little too much. She was only human. She was also unbelievably happy. "There's nothing to forgive, Cabot."

For the first time since he'd walked in here today, the tension drained from his face and he smiled. "I'm glad."

"But I'm curious. What happened after I left?"

"Besides the fact that I missed you like crazy?" He looked out the window, a thoughtful expression on his face. "The community I've always loved and counted on to be there for me did exactly that. The people at the diner were sure I'd lost my mind. Caroline said, and I quote, that if I didn't go after you, I was a damn fool. And dense as they come. Tyler told me girls aren't my best event."

She laughed. "Did he really?"

"Oh, yeah. Kind of pathetic when your eight-year-old son knows more about women than you do." He grinned. "The thing is that all of them were just saying what I already knew deep down inside. I fell for you hard, fast and forever."

"Does Tyler know where you are?"

Cabot nodded. "I told him I was going to find you and tell you I love you. He gave me a hug and a high five. He misses you, Kate."

She still remembered the sad look on his little face when she'd said goodbye. For all her worry about him getting attached to her, she was really glad he cared because he'd stolen her heart. It was nice to know he was in her corner, along with the rest of Blackwater Lake. "I feel like the luckiest person in the whole world."

He shook his head. "I'm the lucky one. Of all the diners in all the world, you walked into the Grizzly Bear and answered my Help Wanted ad. At the time, I didn't know how much I needed you. Now I do."

She trailed a finger down the fancy buttons on his crisp dress shirt. "So, why *do* you look like you just ran out on a wedding?"

"I hope I'm running *to* one." He tugged her close and put his arm around her waist, holding her against him. "Will you marry me, Kate?"

"Yes." Her heart filled to overflowing. "I love you, too, Cabot. And this is one wedding I won't run away from."

"Good."

"How does Ty feel about us getting married?"

"I didn't tell him about proposing to you in case the answer was no. But I have a sneaking suspicion that he'll be pretty happy." He kissed her mouth softly, then said, "He set us up, remember?"

"Yes, he did." She sighed. "Nothing would make me happier than spending the rest of my life with you and Ty and putting down roots on the ranch."

"I'm glad."

"And it's all because you took pity on me and gave me a job."

"Best decision I ever made." This time when he kissed her it was long and thorough.

Andrea would have to fix her makeup, but Kate didn't have the will to worry about that. All she cared about was spending the rest of her life with Cabot.

Epilogue

On the chilly October evening Kate got married, she wasn't nervous at all. It was a sunset event and couldn't have been more different from her last wedding. Except for one thing. She did run again—straight into Cabot's arms.

Their wedding was a small affair at Cabot's house on the ranch with her family and their closest friends in attendance. Ty was the best man and ring bearer. Cabot teased that it was a twofer. Kate's sister, Amy Scott, was maid of honor. It was casual, personal and perfect.

They said their vows in front of the big stone fireplace in the great room. After the minister from the local church pronounced them husband and wife, Cabot cupped her face in his hands and smiled with satisfaction, then proceeded to kiss her soundly.

He reluctantly pulled back and looked down when Ty tugged on his suit coat. "What is it, son?"

"When do I get to make my best-man speech?"

Cabot looked at her. "What do you think? Is there a specific schedule?"

She shook her head. "Do you want to do that now, Ty?"

"Yes."

"Okay. We just need to get champagne poured and make sure everyone has a glass." She looked at her brother. "Zach, can you handle that?"

He nodded. "Mom, Dad, Amy, can you give me a hand?"

The Scott family mobilized in the adjacent kitchen to pop corks and pour the bubbly. Tyler and his friend C.J had apple cider. Kate didn't want anyone left out of the toast.

Finally she and Cabot stood with the cheerfully crackling fire behind them and flutes of champagne in their hands. Ty was beside his father, and everyone was quietly gathered around to hear his words. Kate knew Cabot had talked to his son about this moment, but they had no idea what the little boy was going to say.

"My dad told me to thank everyone for coming. So, thanks." He looked around at Caroline and Nolan. The Crawfords, who owned the diner. Sydney McKnight and her father, Tom. The wedding guests faded to a blur as she concentrated on this sweet, precocious child who was now her son.

"Dad said I should say what I feel." He hesitated a moment, as if trying to figure it out. "I'm really glad Kate didn't marry that other guy. I'm glad she ran away and came to Blackwater Lake. My dad told me she makes him really happy and he loves her." He glanced up at them and grinned. "And I'm real glad that she's my mom now. I love her, too."

Kate's eyes filled with happy tears when she bent to hug him. "That was the best best-man speech ever. It was beautiful, Ty."

"Then why are you cryin'?"

She sniffled. "Because what you said was wonderful, and I'm so happy."

Spontaneous applause and laughter erupted

from everyone present, but Ty still looked confused.

Cabot put a hand on the boy's shoulder. "Kate loved it."

"Really?" The boy looked skeptical.

"Really." Her husband met her gaze and said with conviction, "You just have to trust."

"Okay." Ty shrugged and then gave her a pleading look. "Can I go play with C.J. now?"

"Of course. Go have fun."

He didn't waste any time and disappeared while the adults moved close, forming an unofficial receiving line to offer congratulations and wishes for a long, happy life. Sydney McKnight was the last one and gave her a big hug.

The pretty brunette smiled. "See, I told you the very first time we met that Cabot was sweet on you."

"When my brother's truck broke down."

Syd glanced at the brother in question, who was now talking with Cabot. "He's not hard on the eyes."

"Please, I beg you, don't have a crush on my brother."

"It was just an observation. I've sworn off men." Syd held up a hand in protest. "But why the warning? You're deliriously happy with your handsome rancher and I'm glad for you. But when people are sappy in love, they try to fix up their friends. Is there something wrong with me?"

"Absolutely not. Any man would be lucky to have you." Kate was adamant.

"At least one guy didn't think so."

"Then he was stupid. But if Zach broke your heart, it might affect our friendship."

"That wouldn't happen," Syd guaranteed. "As your husband so eloquently said to his son, you have to trust."

"Husband." Kate sighed dreamily. "I love the sound of that."

She met Cabot's gaze and saw the tender expression he wore only for her. He was no longer that cynical, guarded man who wouldn't believe in forever. Who'd ever have thought anyone would use *Cabot* and *trust* in the same sentence?

Just a little while ago, Kate had vowed that he would never have cause to regret trusting her, and he'd made the same promise. She'd expect nothing less from her hero, the rancher who took her in.

* * * * *